JAMIE  SMART'S

FLEMBER

THE CRYSTAL CAVES

David Fickling Books

31 Beaumont Street
Oxford OX1 2NP, UK

Flember: The Crystal Caves
is a
DAVID FICKLING BOOK

First published in Great Britain in 2020 by
David Fickling Books,
31 Beaumont Street,
Oxford, OX1 2NP

Text & Illustrations © Jamie Smart, 2020
Colouring of inside artwork by Emily Kimbell

978-1-78845-148-2

1 3 5 7 9 10 8 6 4 2

Papers used by David Fickling Books are from
well-managed forests and other responsible sources.

MIX
Paper from
responsible sources
FSC
www.fsc.org   FSC® C018072

DAVID FICKLING BOOKS Reg. No. 8340307

A CIP catalogue record for this book is
available from the British Library.

Printed and bound in Great Britain by Clays, Ltd, Elcograf S.p.A

Everything hungers for something.

FLEMBER

THE MYSTERIOUS,
MAGICAL POWER THAT FLOWS
THROUGH ALL LIVING THINGS!

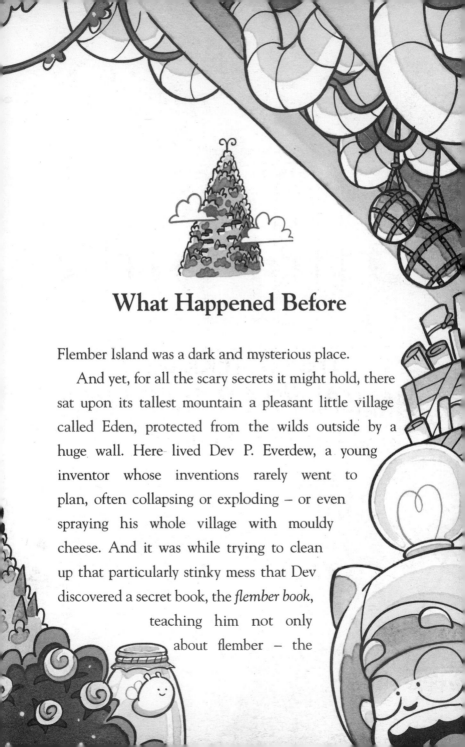

What Happened Before

Flember Island was a dark and mysterious place.

And yet, for all the scary secrets it might hold, there sat upon its tallest mountain a pleasant little village called Eden, protected from the wilds outside by a huge wall. Here lived Dev P. Everdew, a young inventor whose inventions rarely went to plan, often collapsing or exploding – or even spraying his whole village with mouldy cheese. And it was while trying to clean up that particularly stinky mess that Dev discovered a secret book, the *flember book*, teaching him not only about flember – the

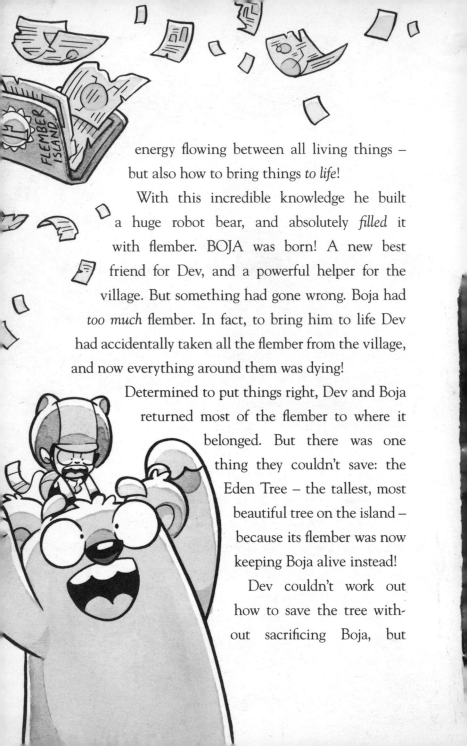

energy flowing between all living things –
but also how to bring things *to life*!

With this incredible knowledge he built
a huge robot bear, and absolutely *filled* it
with flember. BOJA was born! A new best
friend for Dev, and a powerful helper for the
village. But something had gone wrong. Boja had
too much flember. In fact, to bring him to life Dev
had accidentally taken all the flember from the village,
and now everything around them was dying!

Determined to put things right, Dev and Boja
returned most of the flember to where it
belonged. But there was one
thing they couldn't save: the
Eden Tree – the tallest, most
beautiful tree on the island –
because its flember was now
keeping Boja alive instead!

Dev couldn't work out
how to save the tree without sacrificing Boja, but

then the flember book revealed
one last secret. A map, hidden between its words,
illuminated by the power of
flember itself!

But where could this
map lead, and what
might Dev and Boja
find there . . . ?

4

BER TRANSFERENCE
ORROWING ONE TO FUEL THE OTHER)

19
3:

e have already established the flember
rocess as it occurs in nature - what we ca
CALE. It is constant, infinitesimal, splitti
rees. It is relentless, and if we could hear
deafening. We don't consider it a great
however, to want to try and REPLICA
smaller scale, of course, but still To cop

1
An Early Start

Dev P. Everdew stood on the front steps of his house.

His breath curled out into the morning air.

He was ill-dressed for this time of day. The night had been particularly chilly, with no sign yet of the sun, and goose bumps ran along the length of his arms. His large, cat-eared helmet kept his head warm, and his long orange scarf protected his neck, but he'd

rushed outside without grabbing so much as a coat.

Just a backpack, slung over one shoulder.

And the flember book under his arm.

'Come onnnnn, Boja . . .' he whispered.

The house creaked.

A big red paw squeezed out through the doorway. It gripped the stone steps and then, with some effort, pulled a big red face after it. A bulging eye, then a shiny black nose, then, as if the effort was all too much, Boja stopped halfway, and he fell asleep.

'Boja!' Dev knelt down beside Boja's big red ear. 'Boja, wake up!'

Boja grunted. His eye opened. A big goofy smile

spread across his mouth. Then he started pushing again. The other eye popped through the doorway, the other ear, the whole head. A pause for breath. The shoulders. The chest. Another pause, while Dev watched to make sure the house wasn't rising off the ground. One more push. A fart, a giggle, the bum – and then OUT.

'Waffles!' Boja declared, standing up straight as all his mechanical joints click-clicked back into place. His big black nose niff-niff-niffed the air, searching for the faintest scent of waffles, but all it caught was the smell of the Spindletree Forest behind them. 'No waffles,' he grumbled, clutching his belly.

His belly grumbled back in agreement.

'Oh, we're looking for something FAR more exciting than waffles.' Dev chuckled. 'Quickly now, before everyone else wakes up!'

Together they walked away from the house. Across the broken stone bridge. Up the path. Between all the blue-roofed buildings of Middle Eden and out, onto the moonlit cobbles of the marketplace.

The stores were closed.

The streets were empty.

'HUNNNN-GRYYYYY!' Boja moaned loudly in Dev's ear.

'Boja, keep your voice down! We don't want to wake everyone up!'

Boja frowned a frown so big it almost didn't fit on his face. Then, suddenly, his nose started to twitch. His nostrils flared. His whole head spun the rest of his body around on the spot. He had caught a scent, a sweet, sugary scent, and it pulled him like a fish on a hook. Down, through the tightly packed alleys. A sharp left, a hard right, Boja's feet barely touching the ground as his shiny black nose dragged the rest of his body along behind it.

Finally, he screeched to a halt outside Arnold's Waffle Shop.

Boja stared lovingly at the empty, unwashed bowls, the waffley crumbs on the ground, the bins filled with half-eaten waffle bits.

And his tongue drooped down to his belly.

'The shop's . . . not . . . open yet,' Dev panted as he caught up. 'Arnold will still be asleep!'

'I like waffles.' Boja grinned, his grin now grinning as big as his frown had once frowned.

'Of course you do, they're delicious.' Dev leant his shoulder into Boja's stomach, slowly heaving the greedy bear back towards the main road. 'And soon, SOON, you can have all the waffles you—'

'BEHHHHHH!' A loud bleat interrupted them both. A little goat, lying guard on the large stone steps of the Great Hall, jumped onto his tottery legs and waggled his fluffy tail.

'FEVVUS!' Boja squealed.

'Quietly!' Dev whispered, lifting a finger to his lips.

Boja nodded. Then he rose onto his tiptoes and tippy-tippy-tiptoed as quietly as he could towards Fervus. It swiftly became apparent, however, that Boja had even less control over his body when tiptoeing than when his feet were flat to the ground. He started leaning to the left, more to the left, and e-e-even more to the left. Soon he had missed Fervus the goat completely and was heading towards a stack of chicken crates.

As he neared, the chickens started to wake, their sleepy 'bukawk's rising in volume until CRUNCH! Boja's foot went through one of the crates. CRUNCH! The other foot into another, until he lost his balance completely and flumped into the whole pile, an avalanche of BUKAWK-ing chickens spilling out across the road.

'So much for doing this quietly!' Dev sighed.

Suddenly Boja was up again, crates wedged not only onto his feet like a big pair of ridiculous shoes, but also on his paws and his head, while great clumps of chicken feathers spilled out from his nose. 'BUKAWKKK!' he screeched, before breaking into fits of giggles.

'Boja, please!' Dev implored, pushing the loud, clomping chicken-bear along the road. 'Can we just get through the village without causing any more *noise*?'

Boja lifted a crate to his head as if saluting. 'Bukawk,' he whispered, striding purposefully on, at least for the first few steps. Then he tripped, stumbled and collapsed onto his face. His bottom rolled over his head, then his head rolled over his bottom, as suddenly the slope of the road steepened and Boja started tumbling down it at speed.

Dev ran along behind, throwing himself towards Boja as if he could drag him to a stop. Instead, he was bundled up too, crumpled inside a mass of fur, feather and disintegrating chicken crates.

'B-B-B-JUH!' he shouted through a mouthful of Boja's belly.

'HU-BUB, HU-BUB, HU-BUB BUB BUB!' Boja gurgled, bouncing past the houses, the trees, out onto the dusty path and towards the Wall. And though the Wall – a seemingly endless line of tree trunks tightly stacked along Eden's perimeter – was immense, it still wobbled a little under the weight of a giant chicken-bear crashing into it.

Boja was caught by the thick, thorny bramble bush that grew along the base of the Wall, but his momentum propelled Dev high enough to grab onto one of its thick metal rivets. Then he reached for another, and another, eventually hauling himself up to the very top where he sat between the Wall's spikes and took a moment to catch his breath.

And a moment longer to hold down his stomach.

'That's one way of getting through the village,' he wheezed.

A cold breeze rippled up the back of his neck. He turned, leaning away from Eden and peering over the other side of the Wall, down into the rustling shadows of the mountainside. Down into the *Wildening*. His pulse quickened. He lifted his head, his eyes nervously following the treetops across the endless darkness of Flember Island.

And a heavy sense of dread bubbled up inside his stomach.

He gulped. 'I really hope we're doing the right thing.'

2
The Map

'DEV! GET DOWN FROM THERE!'

Santoro jogged down the road towards the Wall. His purple hair was ruffled. His feet were bare. He wore nothing but a night tunic and a *furious* expression on his face. 'You . . . you really think you can squeeze a huge *bear* out through the house like no one will notice?'

Dev sighed in relief at the sight of his brother. 'Santoro!'

'Get DOWN!'

'Let me explain!'

'NO!' Santoro growled, marching through the trail of broken chicken crates. 'You nearly destroyed this whole village only *yesterday*. You and that big red lump!'

Boja, who was currently covered in feathers and upside down with his bum squished into his own face, quietly bukawk-ed with indignation. 'But we *forgave* you, Dev. The whole village, we forgave you, we all went to sleep and everything was fine. It was FINE.'

'I found a map!' Dev beamed. 'It's hidden in the pages of this book!'

Santoro wasn't looking at the book. His eyes were locked firmly onto Dev. And he wasn't slowing down.

'Boja, er, maybe you should come up here,' Dev suggested. 'Come up, Boja. Quickly! COME UP! COMEUPCOMEUP!'

Boja scrambled upright, clawing through the thorns and the bracken, grabbing onto the Wall's rivets and using them to heave his considerable weight to the top. He huddled, precariously, behind Dev.

'Let's show him the map.' Dev grinned, pulling out the first few pages. 'Boja, would you mind?'

Boja meeped excitedly, lifted one of his paws and pressed a finger against the first page. A gentle glow of flember started to spin around his fingertip. Sparkles of blue light wafted down upon the paper. *Flember!* It struck invisible lines, symbols, letters, all hidden between the words, all now lighting up as if they had been drawn in starlight.

Dev had spent most of the night studying these glowing pages, but his heart still swelled at the sight of them. 'The lines have been drawn with traces of flemberthyst dust, so they're invisible until flember passes through them.' He beamed. 'At first I thought it was a map of the island. See? On these first few pages here's Eden, here's the Wall, and then here's everything beyond it. But then I realized it's not showing us what's *on* the island. It's showing us what's *underneath* it!'

Santoro threw himself into the brambles. Its thorns tore long thin scratches across his arms, his face, digging into his bare feet as he tried to claw his way through. 'Get DOWN from there!' he shouted.

'But it's a map of the *Flember Stream*!' Dev shoved the next couple of pages against Boja's finger. 'Oh, Santoro, Nonna showed me the Flember Stream a couple of days ago! It's the most beautiful thing ever! It's like a huge, sparkling river deep underneath the ground, a river which carries all of the island's flember around from one living thing to another.'

He remembered how magical it had felt when his grandmother Ventillo – his *Nonna* – had shown him a hidden little cave and together they had watched waves of flember, rising and falling, washing back and forth through all the flemberthyst crystals.

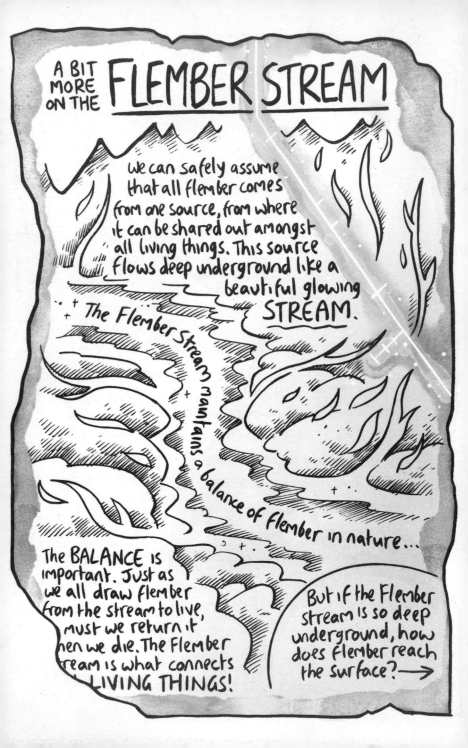

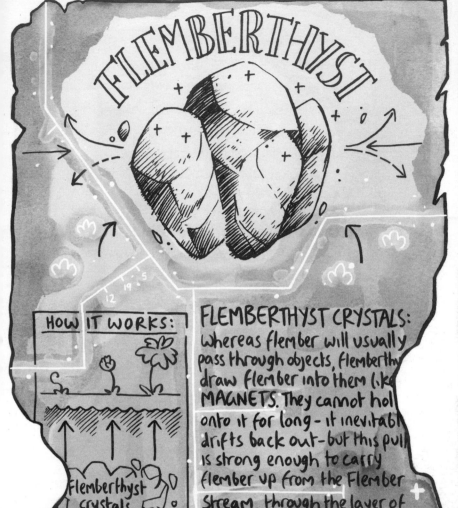

FLEMBERTHYST

HOW IT WORKS:

Flemberthyst crystals

FLEMBER STREAM

FLEMBERTHYST CRYSTALS:

Whereas flember will usually pass through objects, flemberthy draw flember into them like MAGNETS. They cannot hol onto it for long - it inevitabl drifts back out - but this pull is strong enough to carry flember up from the Flember Stream, through the layer of flemberthyst crystals we find beneath the soil, and then out into the world. Once it finds a seed, a it can bless wi

'If I could just reach the Flember Stream again, then maybe I could fix what I broke.'

Santoro finally gave up, his body tangled and suspended in the thick brambles. 'What did you break?' he grumbled. 'What are you TALKING about?'

Dev pointed along Eden's main road. Past the marketplace. The Old Woods. Across Shady Acres and all the way to the top. All the way up to where the most beautiful tree in existence had once stood.

Now just a twisted, blackened trunk remained.

Dev sighed. 'The Eden Tree needs flember to bring it back to life. Boja can carry flember, more than he needs for his own body, so if he could just borrow a little from the Flember Stream and carry it up there, put it back inside the tree, then everything would be OK again!'

'BORROW flember?' Santoro cried. 'Dev, you messing about with flember is what caused all this trouble in the first place!'

'Exactly!' A lump rose in Dev's throat. 'My flember experiments broke the Eden Tree. It's *my* fault it's dead. Every time people look at it they'll say it was me, Dev P. Everdew, the *terrible inventor* who left it like that.' He sniffled back tears. 'Well, it's *me* who has to fix it. And I can't sit around waiting for the Flember Stream to come all the way back up the mountain again. I have to go and find it *myself*.'

'See, there's a place on the island called Darkwater. A town, maybe. It's just at the bottom of our mountain – it really doesn't look very far at all.' Dev spoke fast in the hope his brother wouldn't be able to shout over him. 'Usually the Flember Stream runs way too deep for anyone to see, but the map says there's a point in Darkwater where it comes close to the surface!'

'You can't go over this Wall,' Santoro yelled. 'The WILDENING lies beyond the Wall! You wouldn't dare go into the Wildening!'

Dev shuddered at the memory of all the stories he'd heard about the Wildening. The wurdelsnumpf, the grobbits and all the other terrifying monsters, creatures and beasties which supposedly lurked amongst the shadows. 'I . . . I'll be fine,' he stuttered. 'I'll have Boja with me! He'll keep me safe!'

'SNNNNKKK!' Boja snored. He had somehow managed to fall asleep. His paw slumped away from the pages Dev was holding as his flember crackled back around his fingertips, then sank beneath his fur.

The glowing map faded.

'What about MUM?' Santoro replied. 'She'll be so worried about you!'

'I left a note!' Dev replied, closing the book. 'For her, for *all* of you! It's in my workshop. It explains what I'm doing, why I'm doing it, and that we'll only be gone for a couple of days. Then we'll come right back and fix the Eden Tree!'

A surprisingly loud 'BEHHHHHHHH' interrupted him. He looked up to see Fervus the goat powering excitedly down the road, a variety of window shutters clonk-clonking open around him as bleary-eyed villagers peered out of their homes to see what all the noise was about.

At the sound of Fervus bleating Boja squealed himself awake. He sat bolt upright only to instantly lose his balance, his eyes bulging wide with panic as he disappeared over the other side of the Wall. His paws reached out, desperately clawing for something to grab onto.

They found the end of Dev's scarf.

Eden swung out of sight as Dev was yanked sharply backwards, tumbling down the Wall and crashing  through a canopy of tree branches before landing on Boja's huge, pillowy stomach.

'HOOOOOOOF!' Boja wheezed from one end, while a honking fart escaped from the other. Dev slid down onto the soft, dew-soaked grass, checking his bear for any injuries, and brushing away the last of his feathers.

'DEV, DON'T GO!' Santoro's voice called out from the other side of the Wall. 'It's DANGEROUS out there. It's SO DANGEROUS!'

More voices rose up around Santoro. Other villagers who must have seen Dev and Boja disappear over the Wall. 'Lad, you must be crazy!' someone yelled. 'The Wildening will chew you up and spit you out!'

Somewhere further up the hill, the bells of the Great Hall started to chime.

The whole village would be waking up.

'We'll be OK!' Dev shouted back. 'Me and Boja, we'll look out for each other!'

He gripped tightly onto Boja's red thumb, as a gentle pulse of flember coursed across his hand.

It felt warm.

Reassuring.

He smiled up at the big red bear.

'We'll look out for each other,' he whispered.

3
Beyond the Wall

The path leading away from Eden was so rocky and overgrown it would have been hard to call it a path at all, were a row of willow trees not lining either side. Their low hanging leaves brushed gently against Dev's face, then flapped into Boja's, before the path opened up and there, in the light of an early morning sun, the whole mountainside stretched out below them.

Dev nervously glanced around, scared of what might pounce out at them from the Wildening. Boja, however, didn't seem that fussed. He was far too distracted by his own rumbling stomach.

'No . . . waffles,' he grumbled.

'I don't think they have waffle shops out here,' Dev replied. 'But if I see one, I'll let you know.'

Boja's stomach-rumbles accompanied their climb down the mountain. Most of the time it was a long, groaning noise, but sometimes it boilked, sometimes it even sque-e-eaked, like a terrible song played by too many terrible instruments.

By the time they reached the edge of the forest, it had become a little too much for Dev to bear.

'Boja, your belly is so *noisy!*'

'HU-U-U-UNGRY,' Boja whined, flinging his head back for maximum effect.

'Well, here, what about . . . this?' Dev reached into a withered bush and plucked an overripe bobbleberry. It looked small, wrinkled and tough, and even a little bit hairy.

Boja sniffed it suspiciously, then popped it into his mouth. It crunched loudly between his teeth as if he was chewing a pebble. 'Not . . . food,' he moaned, fishing the half-chewed bobbleberry from between his lips and plopping it back onto the bush.

'Mum used to tell us these stories about how if we didn't eat all of our dinner, she'd scrape our plates over the Wall and into the Wildening,' Dev said. 'And then these horrible creatures called groakers – like greasy little gnomes, with huge bellies but tiny thin legs – they'd scuttle out of the darkness and they'd stuff the scraps into their mouths. And then they'd be hungry for more, so they'd climb over the Wall, and they'd come and find us, and they'd start eating us too, starting from our toes and working their way up!'

He laughed nervously at the memory of it. 'Me and Santoro were so scared. We used to eat everything off our plates, every last crumb!'

He turned to see Boja, his eyes wide, his mouth agape. His trembling paws reached back to grab the half-chewed bobbleberry, as he lifted it to his mouth and reluctantly swallowed it.

'Probably for the best,' Dev said, tucking the flember book under his arm and slipping his backpack from his shoulders. 'But you don't just need to eat old bobble-berries, Boja. I was going to save this till later but, well, I packed us some *supplies*.'

The thought of something decent to eat made Boja's nose twitch excitedly. 'SUPPLIES!' he yipped, not

RASSLECLOCK

necessarily knowing what
the word meant.

'All right, all right!'

FIBBULATOR

Dev laughed, rooting around in
his backpack and pulling out a strange,
lumpy-looking device cobbled together from old bits
of wood. 'Oh. That's my Fibbulator. Hang on.'

He cast the Fibbulator aside and reached in for
something else.

What he pulled out
was a cube, short poles
sticking out from its
sides and a light bip-bip-
bipping at one end. 'Rassleclock,' Dev

BIMCOCKLE

RIPPLYBOLLOP

muttered, pulling more things out of the
backpack. 'Bimcockle. Ripplybollop.
Optylopops. A spring-loaded Fisplestaw.
But no . . . food . . . at all.'

OPTYLOPOPS

He scooped the tools back inside his
backpack, then slid the flember book in

between them. 'I'm sorry, Boja.
I packed in a hurry. I was too
excited. I must have . . . *forgotten*
. . . to pack the freeze-dried waffles.'

SPRING-LOADED
FISPLESTAW

Boja flung his arms up in total

29

desperation. 'HUNNNGRYYYY!' he cried, waggling his paws as if summoning waffles from the sky. Gentle sparks of flember danced out from his fingertips, sparks which caught upon the branches above him and PLINK-PLINK-PLINK-ed out a number of tiny pink flower buds.

An idea flickered inside Dev's brain.

'Boja, what if you gave a little bit of your flember to the *bobbleberry bush*?'

Boja lowered his arms, drawing his flember away from the branch as its little flowers wilted away. He stepped cautiously towards the bobbleberry bush. Then he reached out a paw and pointed a finger down upon its roots. Bright, sparkling flember wisped across his fur. It crackled through the stalk, spiralling out along the leaves, the whole bush suddenly shining with a beautiful blue glow.

And then, to Boja's utter delight, a plump round bobbleberry PLIP-ed out from inside. And another. PLIP! PLIP! PLIP PLIP PLIP!

Boja reached in, plucked a shiny bobbleberry and slipped it in his mouth. As it burst between his teeth, his whole face rolled up in pleasure.

'It's your own flember you're eating.' Dev smiled. 'So it's not like you're losing any of it. Bring the plant with you. We've still quite a way to go.'

Boja wrenched the bush out from the ground, carrying it like a big glowing candyfloss. Every few seconds he plucked another bobbleberry and for every bobbleberry picked, a new one grew in its place.

Dev watched him enviously. He was hungry too! But he knew he couldn't eat a single bobbleberry from Boja's bush, not without taking a little bit of Boja's flember with it. He looked, instead, for what other food the Wildening might offer, and he found a few wild vegetables he recognized. Peppers, for example, as well as flonions and sprickets. Like the bobbleberries had been, they too were all withered and overripe. Tiny. Wrinkled. A bit hairy. Still, he plucked a few of each and stuffed them inside his pocket, chewing on a spricket skin until he could find anything better.

PEPPER

MINI CAULIFLOWER

FLONION

As they walked deeper into the forest the ground became more uneven. The trees here grew upon a slope, nothing but mud and rock between them, and when rain started to pitter-patter through the leaves the mud turned into a wet, squelchy gloop.

'Maybe we should find somewhere to shelter,' Dev said, a cold raindrop hanging from the tip of his nose. 'Somewhere dry.'

SPRICKETS

Boja, his cheeks stuffed full with bobbleberries,

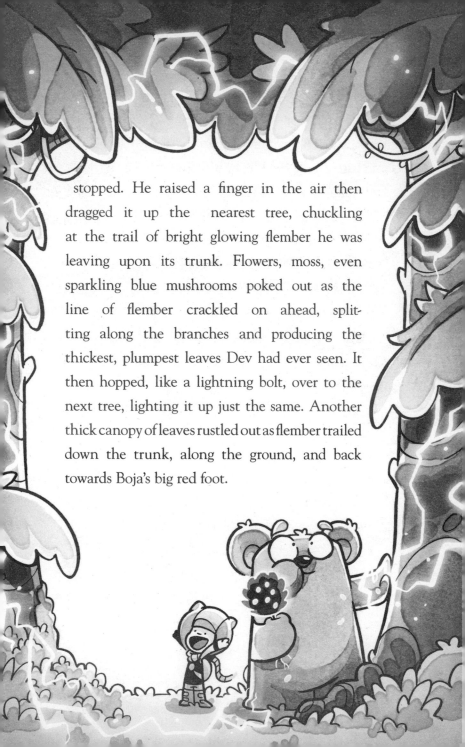

stopped. He raised a finger in the air then dragged it up the nearest tree, chuckling at the trail of bright glowing flember he was leaving upon its trunk. Flowers, moss, even sparkling blue mushrooms poked out as the line of flember crackled on ahead, splitting along the branches and producing the thickest, plumpest leaves Dev had ever seen. It then hopped, like a lightning bolt, over to the next tree, lighting it up just the same. Another thick canopy of leaves rustled out as flember trailed down the trunk, along the ground, and back towards Boja's big red foot.

'No more . . . rain.' Boja grinned, plucking a few more bobbleberries as he sat beneath their umbrella of leaves. Dev sat down beside him. He beamed with pride at his brilliant robot bear, nuzzling his head into Boja's soft fur, and listening to the rain as it pattered down outside their little camp.

'We're making good progress already,' Dev said.

'Bobbleberries,' Boja chomped.

'Exactly, Boja. You have bobbleberries. I have you. And together we'll be in Darkwater before we know it.'

He let out a wide yawn.

'The Wildening's not scary at all,' he murmured. Then his eyes started to close, and he drifted off into a deep, deep sleep.

4
Where it all Went Wrong

Dev awoke, shivering. He had been enjoying a dream about duck eggs on wildertoast and savouring every crunch, every imaginary squish between his teeth. That is, until a raindrop plopped down upon his nose, and suddenly he was miles away from the warmth of his mum's kitchen.

He was back in a cold, dark forest.

And he was alone.

Wherever Boja had gone he'd taken his flember with him, and their shelter of leaves had withered back into the branches. Now there was nothing to hold the rain back. Within seconds a few drops became a downpour, lashing against Dev's skin as if scolding him, pounding at the mud as he struggled to stand.

'BOJA!' he shouted, his voice instantly swallowed by a great rumble of thunder. Huge, swaying sheets of rain filled the skies. Dev tightened his scarf around his neck, wedged his helmet even tighter onto his head and peered through the darkness. 'BOJA WHERE ARE YOU?'

And then he saw it.

A snoring lump of red fur sliding down the slope.

'BOJA!' Dev threw himself into the mud as if it were a waterslide. He tumbled down the slope at speed, spinning, rolling and gasping for breath between mouthfuls of thick, gloopy mud.

Then he remembered something.

The Portable Airbag he'd installed inside his backpack! He clawed in desperation at the front hoop of his straps, hoping the airbag might inflate, that it might at least keep his head out of the mud.

But it didn't work. Nothing came out.

Instead he slammed into Boja's mud-soaked backside and awoke Boja with a start. 'GNUUUUHHH-LMPH!' the wet bear wailed. Dev gasped, his head bobbing above the surface just long enough to exclaim something similar, as Boja quickly, instinctively, drew an arm around Dev's waist.

And Dev could see the sky again.

He saw lightning crackle across the clouds as if it was tearing them apart. He saw each and every raindrop, lit up like a million tiny shards of glass. For such an almighty storm it all looked so . . . *beautiful.*

Suddenly a huge wave of cold, sloppy mud crashed down upon them both, wrenching Dev from Boja's grip and dragging him away. Dev flailed around, his hands desperate for something to hold onto, but all he could see was mud. All he could hear was mud.

Then, without warning, all the mud spilled away from beneath him.

And he splashed down into a lake.

He pulled his head above the waters, gasping great lungfuls of air, looking frantically around for any sign of Boja. Then he dived back under, straining to see a bulging eye, a furry bum, even just a wisp of red fur through the murk.

But nothing.

Only when his chest felt like it was ready to burst did he kick back to the surface. He grabbed onto a bobbing lump of bark and floated himself towards the water's edge. Then pulled himself up slimy green tree roots and hauled himself onto land.

A slow, wet grinding noise sounded from behind him.

And then . . . FLOOMP! The Portable Airbag finally deployed. Dev's backpack ballooned out around him, sending his tools, and the flember book, spinning into the air.

He collapsed, exhausted, on top of it.

'Boja, where are you?' he whimpered.

Something sticky crawled across his skin. He looked down to see dark slimy leeches on his arms. 'YEARGH!' he yelped, plucking

and flicking them off. With a renewed urgency he squished the inflatable airbag back inside his backpack, gathered up his tools and the book, and stuffed them in with it.

He felt a sharp pain in his neck. He pinched at the cause of it – a small round insect. It had a large pointy stinger protruding from its backside. Another insect plomped down onto his hand, and stung him too. Then they were all around him. Thin, buzzing ones. Wide, flappy ones. Bright, glowing ones. They FRRP-ed and FWWP-ed and ZWIPP-ed around him, their hums ringing in his ears, the sky darkening under the weight of them all.

Dev ran from the water's edge, and into the shadow of the trees. The ground became boggy. Sticky,

squelchy mud gripped around his ankles, pulling on his legs until he stumbled face first into it. With a loud GA-A-A-ASP he heaved himself back out, now covered in brown slop, squelching and parping like some sort of toilet monster.

The insects fluttered their way back to the shore. Toilet monsters, it appeared, were not on their menu tonight.

Dev wiped the mud from his eyes. He stared, bewildered, at his surroundings.

A glowing, uncanny wilderness bustled around him. Dev had studied what grew around Eden but this . . . this was all new. Every flower, plant, fern and tree was completely unknown to him. It was all so utterly beautiful.

And then he heard a noise he recognized.

The roar of a large robot bear.

'BOJA!' he yelled with relief.

The roar came again, this time followed by a bright flash of light through the trees. Dev quickened his pace, battling through long sharp reeds, slipping down muddy banks, clambering over thick tree roots. The lights flashed brighter and quicker in succession.

'BOJA, I'M COMING!'

Fists clenched, teeth gritted, Boja's mud-soaked body heaved with every breath. Flember crackled around him like a storm cloud, while a low, thundering snarl rumbled deep inside his chest.

And then Dev saw what Boja was growling at.

Huge, monstrous-looking shapes lurched and swayed through the trees – what looked like creatures of fur, foliage, antler and horn. They brayed, they screamed and they growled, encircling Boja from the shadows.

And then one of the shapes slinked out. It walked on all fours like a wolf, its body thick and jagged, its skin so dark it looked as if it was made from the night itself. A

red flame burned inside its hollow eye sockets.

It edged towards Boja. Dev opened his mouth to shout, but he was too late – the wolf had already scrambled up Boja's back, its jaw, lined with sharp black teeth, widening to take a bite. Boja, however, was faster, gripping the wolf's head with his huge paw and slamming it down into the ground.

Dev ran to help, only for a second wolf to pounce from the darkness, and sink its teeth into Dev's arm. 'YOWWWW!' he screamed. The dark wolf bit down harder, its muzzle bunched up, its furious red eyes blazing. The pain crackled through Dev's bones until – POW! – a huge red fist slammed into the wolf's ribs, rocketing it high up into the air.

'DEVVVV!' Boja yelled, scooping Dev up into his arms. Then he turned, and he ran as fast as his huge red feet would carry him. He leapt across the uneven ground, bowled through thorny bushes, bundled over fallen trees, until suddenly, without warning, the uneven ground sloped down into an almost vertical drop. Boja skidded, but he couldn't stop in time. He tumbled down the wet mud, curling around Dev like a protective ball as they rolled, and rolled, and rolled down the mountainside. All Dev could hear was the crashing of trees around them, and Boja's golden heart DOOMPF-DOOMPF-DOOMPF-ing so loud it sounded as if it were about to explode.

Then a THUD!

And a CRASH!

The creaking of metal.

More thuds, more crunches, smashes, tinkles and crumples.

Faster they rolled. And faster.

And fasterandfasterandfaster.

At which point Dev's rattled, rolled and frazzled brain could take no more, and he passed out.

5
A Friendly Face

Dev pulled the bed covers up and over his head.

'Just a bit longer, Mum,' he mumbled. 'Then I'll fix the generators. I promise.'

A throbbing pain shot down his arm. He opened his eyes to see the insect stings and the leech marks across his skin. They merged together in a splatter of red, angry blotches.

Three deep, blackened scars sliced between them.

'The dark wolves,' Dev whispered, as the memories slowly bubbled back into his head. 'The Wildening. *Boja!*'

He leapt out of bed, realized he was naked, then leapt back in again, pulling the covers up beneath his chin. This wasn't his *workshop*. This room was cold and empty. Its metal walls peeled with the remains of a pale green wallpaper. Its ceiling hung low and curved. A faint afternoon light shone in through one of its half-shuttered windows.

'Ah, you're awake!' A woman cheerfully poked her head around the doorway. She carried a metal bowl across the room, and placed it down on a small table beside the bed. 'You must be hungry.'

Her thin black lips cracked as she smiled. Her face was almost white, the skin clinging to her cheekbones, her greying hair bundled up and around her head like some over-elaborate pastry. She wore what looked like dirty overalls, torn, folded, and fashioned into a dress.

Dev read the nametag sewn onto it.

'Eat.' She beckoned.

Dev looked inside the bowl. It held a lumpy dollop of steaming green slop with an oily black sheen, looking remarkably similar to something a hufflepig might cough up. It smelled the same too.

Dev shook his head, and pulled the covers further over his nose.

'You'll be hungry soon enough.' Rebecca smiled, sitting by his feet.

'My clothes . . .'

'Oh, we had to take them off. You were all muddy, couldn't have you dirtying up our sheets.'

Suddenly the whole room tilted to one side. Everything, bed and table included, slid a few inches across the metal floor towards a set of double doors. Dev could hear shouting beyond them. He couldn't quite make out the words, but he recognized them as being rather rude.

'Your . . . your friend told me your name was *Dev*.' Rebecca caught Dev's panicked stare.

'Boja! Is he . . .'

'He's fine, he's OK.'

'Where . . . where is he?' Dev bundled the sheets up around himself, and stepped onto the cold floor. As he did, his legs wobbled and he crumpled into a heap.

'Slow down, slow *down*.' Rebecca knelt and helped Dev sit up against the bed. 'Your body has been through a lot. You need to take things slowly.'

'I need Boja,' Dev mumbled.

The room tilted again, further than before. As everything slid towards the double doors, they flung open to reveal a balcony and, just beyond its railings, a large, shiny black nose.

SNIFF! SNIFF SNIFF SNIFF!

A little further, and Boja's wide, bulging eyes appeared.

'DEVVVVVV!' Boja squealed.

'Boja!' Dev's heart swelled at the sight of him. 'Are you OK? Are you hurt?'

'Hungry.' Boja's eyes locked onto the bedside table, and the bowl of stew upon it.

'This stew is for DEV.' Rebecca gripped the bedpost with one hand, and Dev with the other. 'He's not well.'

The whole room lurched again, sliding the table out

bowl of black and green muck tumbled over and towards Boja's wide-open mouth.

'That stew is for DEV!' Rebecca shouted so angrily it made Boja's mouth snap shut. The bowl slapped between his eyes and slowly slid down onto his nose. From somewhere below, the rude words started again. Boja smiled sheepishly, disappearing from sight as the room rose back up into a horizontal position.

Rebecca composed herself and patted down her overalls. 'He wouldn't eat until he knew you were OK.' She tutted. 'I guess he knows you're OK now.'

Dev carefully lifted himself back onto the bed. 'What's he doing out there?'

Rebecca picked up Dev's clothes, helmet and backpack from a chair on the other side of the room, and she placed them on the bed. 'He's helping. When you're ready, get dressed, come downstairs, and see.'

6
The Village

As soon as Rebecca had left the room, Dev shuffled over to his backpack and opened it up. He pulled out the flember book. Its cracked blue cover was muddy, but much to his relief the pages inside were still dry. He ran a finger across the large golden F on its cover.

Flember prickled warmly against his skin.

The tools he'd packed hadn't fared so well. The Fibbulator sloshed full of dirty brown water. The Bimcockle too. The Rassleclock bipped once and then burst into flames, while the Ripplybollop, Optylopops and even the spring-loaded Fisplestaw had all been crumpled together into one big lump of junk.

'Maybe my helmet still works.' Dev lifted up his

helmet and plopped it onto his head. He pulled the chin-straps. A little hatch opened at the top and more muddy water spilled out, followed by a groaning cluster of broken metal arms and a fizzing, popping light bulb.

And then, a snail.

Dev plucked it between his fingers and carefully placed it on the wall. He piled his broken tools beside the bed, slipped the book back inside his backpack, put on his trousers, vest and his boots, and finally he wrapped his scarf around his neck.

'At least Boja's here,' he muttered, standing on two wobbly legs, pulling a soggy, withered pepper from his pocket and chewing on it as he staggered out of the room.

Dev stepped onto a balcony overhanging a huge round hall. Its walls were covered with twisted pipes from floor to ceiling, all of them leading up and into a bulging stalactite of ovens, canisters and tubes which had been cobbled together and thinned into nozzles. Whatever this contraption was, it hung proudly down in the middle of everything, ropes trailing out from it like a spider's web.

Over each rope had been draped a tapestry of dirty, torn canvas sheets, hanging like makeshift tents.

It felt to Dev as if he was looking down upon the weekend markets of Middle Eden.

'We call this place the Village!' Rebecca called out from behind a circular bar in the middle of the room, as she proudly arranged a bouquet of exhaust pipes in a vase. 'We try our best to make it feel like home, and you are very, *very* welcome here.'

Dev carefully descended the stairs, as an elderly man lurched up to meet him. 'Y'ain't got any gold, have yer?' he snarled. He too wore overalls, most of his nametag ripped off to reveal only a surname. *Grippins*. His boots were torn at the tips, ten large blackened toes on show, and he wore a large floppy hat, which covered all but his mouth. 'Carrying any rings, any trinkets?'

'Any in yer teeth?' Another man flanked Dev, this one even older, even more haggard. His nametag read *Prickles*. He gripped Dev's jaw with one hand, forcing his mouth wide open with the other. 'You must have somethin' in there. Somethin' fer Dahlia.'

'Leave him alone.' Rebecca batted them both away with a broom. 'We finally have a *child* come to town and you miserable old skeletons want to scare him off!' She squeezed Dev's cheeks admiringly, then led him towards the bar. 'Ignore them,' she muttered under her breath. 'They're good people at heart. It's just that things aren't that easy around here, not any more.'

Her eyes drifted to a large painting hanging from the wall.

ALBERT WILBURFORCE

'Not since he's been gone,' she whispered, as if it was an unutterable secret.

A huge, hulking figure stirred at the other end of the bar. She looked weathered. Her head was balding at the sides, her scalp pitted, with a bundle of knotted straw-coloured hair resting upon the top of it.

'The big red one' the figure grumbled. 'What is he?'

Her voice was strange, distorted, as if it was echoing through an old engine.

'B-Boja's a bear,' Dev replied.

The figure snorted. She turned and eyed Dev suspiciously. 'I've never seen a bear like that before. I've never seen a bear talk so much. I've never seen a bear laugh at its own farts. I've never seen a bear so protective of a little boy like *you*.'

A number of thick metal fingers poked out from beneath her shawls as she pushed herself up from her stool. Her whole body creaked and hissed as she moved.

It reminded Dev of the noises the old generators made back in Eden.

'Dev, this is Keeper,' Rebecca said. 'She's the one who caught you both when you came rolling into town.'

'Ah, I just stood in the way,' Keeper grunted, pulling her tatty shawls down over her hands. 'You might wish I'd not bothered. Not now you're stuck in Darkwater like the rest of us.'

Darkwater!

The word spun around in Dev's head before rattling down into his belly.

'Darkwater?' he cried with delight. 'Darkwater's the first place on the map! The first location of the Flember Stream! This is *exactly* where we wanted to be!' He ran across the scuffed floor towards a large set of double doors marked 'EXIT' and flung them open. Daylight hit his eyes. A sharp, cold air filled his lungs. His legs gave way and he collapsed out onto a gangway.

'Do be careful!' Rebecca rushed to help him up. 'I told you already, you need to take things *slowly*.'

As Dev's eyes adjusted he could see his surroundings a little more clearly. The Village, as Rebecca called it, was a curious structure: big and round, like a huge flattened bun riveted together from rusted metal and then perched upon a pile of scrap. The gangway running around it had

been punched with open hatches, and through each of them hung rope ladders. Despite Rebecca's protests Dev clambered towards the nearest hatch, tumbling, haphazardly, down towards the ground.

'BOJA!' he shouted. 'Boja, we've found it! We found Darkwater!'

'Hi, Dev! I'm helping!' Boja stood in the shadow of a towering quarry wall, perched upon a pile of upturned mine carts. The bowl of black and green slop had long since left his nose, slid down his belly, and currently lay splattered across the ground.

'I wouldn't call it *helping*.' A man hung from the gangway. He lifted his welding mask to reveal a face like a puffy red bottom, albeit one with a beard. 'This . . . *bear* of yours keeps making the whole village *dip*! I can hardly weld the supports back together if he doesn't hold it STEADY.'

'Don't worry about Cled,' Rebecca called out, swinging down the rope ladder. 'He'll appreciate your friend's help once it's done. We all will.'

'I'd appreciate him holding it STEADY!' Cled pulled the mask down, and turned his blowtorch back towards the mound. With a face of intense concentration Boja held the Village as steady as he'd ever held anything, until all that concentration forced a tiny little fart from between his buttocks. This brought a chuckle from his lips, and, despite his best efforts, Boja's wobbly arms started shaking the Village again.

'Oh, fine. FINE! It'll have to do,' Cled shouted.

Boja let go of the balcony and clumsily climbed down from his mine carts, throwing out his paws and wrapping Dev into the biggest hug ever hugged.

'I'm so glad you're OK,' Dev whispered, closing his eyes and nuzzling into Boja's red fur. The muffled sound of Boja's golden heart reassuringly doompf-doompf-doompf-ed in his ear once again. 'Wait, *are* you OK?'

He ran some quick diagnostics. Poked a finger into Boja's ear, his nose, his belly. Checked his eyes, his reflexes. Lifted one big red arm, then the other, one leg, then the other. Squeezed at where Boja's organs should be. And for every test he ran, Boja ran the same on him. Poking him, lifting him, flipping him around and squeezing him until finally, succumbing to giggles, and upside down, Dev gave up.

'You seem fine.' Dev smiled with relief. 'Nothing broken, nothing out of place. We fell down a mountain and here you are, still farting.'

'I rolled!' Boja chuckled. 'I rolled and rolled and rolled and rolled!'

'You rolled right across our Village *roof*,' Cled huffed.

'We rolled right through the *Wildening*!' Excitement wobbled in Dev's voice. He gazed up the quarry wall, up to where he could just about see the treetops of the Wildening beyond. 'And you brought us right where we needed to be. First place on the map, Boja. We're in *Darkwater*!'

'DUCKWATER!' Boja yelled.

'WAHOOOO!' Dev cheered.

Rebecca watched the two of them dance wildly on the spot. 'Oh, how lovely.' She smiled wistfully. 'Isn't that lovely, Cled?'

'Hmph,' Cled grumbled. 'You wait till they've seen the rest of Darkwater, see if they're still dancing then.'

7
Darkwater

'Can we take a look around?' Dev asked once the dancing had come to its jiggly, booty-bumping close.

Rebecca winced. 'I'm not sure that's a good idea, Dev. You're not well – you're still recovering from your journey.'

'Ah, let them look,' Cled sniffed. 'It'll keep the bear out of my beard for a little while.'

'But they—'

'Let them *look*.' Cled cast her a pleading glance.

Rebecca nervously straightened her overalls. 'Well . . . OK. But don't go too far, either of you. It's already quite late in the day and I want you both back by dinner.'

At the sound of the word *dinner* Boja started nodding

enthusiastically. Dev shouted back in agreement. He had already started running ahead, excited to see where the map might have brought them.

A drizzly mist obscured much beyond the Village, but the further Dev went, the more shapes started to emerge. Rusted abandoned vehicles. Half-buried bits of engine. Huge clumps of broken machinery. Pylons as tall as trees, their tops disappearing into the sky. Dev gazed up at the chains strung between them, the lights flashing upon them, the sheer size of everything stretching out around him.

Then, suddenly, he was teetering upon a cliff edge. Boja screeched to a halt behind him, and together they stared down at a scene quite unlike anything they had ever seen before.

The town of Darkwater sat in an enormous quarry, spiralling down through the rock as if it were a screw hole. Each ring was a walled level in itself, a step down to the next, decreasing in size as they descended deeper into the earth. Scattered across the rings, Dev could see a slew of broken machinery and collapsed buildings, masts and platforms left dangling from chains. An assault course of rusting metal, whistling its own eerie song as the wind breezed through its skeletal remains.

What caught his eye most, however, was a tower of rock rising up through the middle of it all. Its sides had been clad with a spiral of platforms and scaffolding, all leading up to a dark, round, domed building.

'Why'd your map bring you here then?' Keeper's metallic voice made Dev jump. 'Look at this place. There's nothing left of Darkwater but a load of old rusting junk.'

'We're looking for the *Flember Stream*.' Dev grinned.

Keeper raised a confused eyebrow.

'The Flember Stream!' Dev insisted. 'It carries flember all around the island! The map says there's a point in Darkwater where it comes close to the surface, close enough that you can see it!'

'Your map brought you here to find flember? In Darkwater?' Keeper's whole body erupted into laughter. 'Dev, have you looked AROUND you?'

Dev pursed his lips and stared across the quarry, at the rust and the ruins, and the hard, dusty ground surrounding it all.

He couldn't see a single tree.

Not even a few sprigs of grass.

No birds were singing, no rivers were trickling, no ferns were rustling.

'There's barely any flember here at *all*,' he gasped, a horribly familiar thought suddenly weighing down upon his shoulders. 'Did . . . did I do this?'

'You?'

'Up in Eden, I . . . I did this experiment, and it worked, it *really* worked . . .' Dev waggled his hands towards Boja. Boja waggled his paws back. 'But it went really wrong too. It started taking all the flember out of our village, the trees died, the ponds dried up, and oh no, oh NO! It reached down here, didn't it? I took all of Darkwater's flember too!'

Keeper stared at the boy in front of her. His eyes glistened. His bottom lip wobbled. 'Dev—' she started.

'I fixed it, though. I put all the flember back in Eden!' Dev sniffled. 'Nearly all of it, I mean. Not the Eden Tree. That's why we came here, looking for a bit more flember!' He kicked at the dusty ground. 'So maybe, while I'm here, I can find some way to fix Darkwater *too*.'

Keeper stared at him with amusement. 'Dev, Darkwater's been like this for YEARS!'

'Years?' Dev puffed his cheeks out with relief. 'So I didn't cause all this? Oh! Oh, PHEW! Something that wasn't my fault!'

Keeper shook her head. 'Come here looking for flember,' she muttered, following a narrow path around the side of the cliff. 'I think you must be holding your map upside down or something.'

'Would you maybe show us around anyway?' Dev called out. 'Just so we can check?'

'Show you around? I'm not a babysitter,' Keeper grumped. 'I've digging to do. I can hardly have you two getting in my way.'

'We can help you dig!' Dev chirped. 'Boja's really strong!'

Keeper turned to look at Boja. Boja grinned back, holding his fists above his head and flexing his muscles.

Keeper's frown sunk even lower. 'FINE,' she snapped. 'Come with me then.'

'YES!' Dev cheered.

'But you mind where you step.'

'We will!'

'And no messing about!'

'No messing about,' Dev nodded. 'We *promise*.'

8
Hibbicus

Dev and Boja followed Keeper around the outer ring of the quarry. The ground became darker. The air became colder. They walked between a mesh of twisted wreckage and discarded machinery, pylons poking out like reeds from a pond, mine carts hanging from chains above them.

A thick smell of grease filled Dev's nostrils, a smell that reminded him of that one time Nonna had deep-fried hairweasels without shaving them first.

'What are all these machines for?' he asked, pinching his nose.

'Mining,' Keeper huffed as she helped pull Dev up and over the remains of a collapsed bridge. 'Darkwater was a

mining town.'

'Mining for what?'

'Rocks. Shiny rocks, if you held them in the right light. But would you *look* at these machines?' Keeper slapped her metal hand against a huge, half-buried drill bit. 'It's been quite some time since anyone's mined *anything*.' She sighed. 'Now all folk here do is salvage along the coast instead.'

She walked on in a tired, mechanical manner, one side of her body lifting up as the other heaved back down. Each footstep clanked loudly in a succession of CLINKs, CLUNKs and ZZZZPs, rolls of steam billowing out from beneath her dragging shawls.

Dev watched her closely. 'Are you a robot?' he finally asked.

Keeper stopped. 'Not a robot,' she huffed, picking up a discarded oil can and swiping a metal finger around inside its cap. She pulled out a goop of thick brown oil and slurped it between her lips. Then she wiped her mouth with her sleeve. 'Don't be so ridiculous.'

Boja looked on, envious at the sight of someone eating something he wasn't.

Soon they reached the outer wall of the quarry. The rock here was black, shiny, and had been weathered into jagged spikes. Something noisy lay beyond it. It hissed, and it roared, and it crashed up against the other side of the wall like a caged animal trying to get through.

Dev and Boja clung nervously onto each other.

'That's just the sea,' Keeper said.

'The SEA?' Dev's heart leapt. He'd only ever seen the sea from high, high up on the mountain, and now here it was on the other side of these rocks. So close he could smell the salt on the breeze. He begged and he pleaded with Keeper to go even closer, but she wouldn't budge.

'You're staying where I can see you,' she replied, kneeling down into the marshy, wet ground and carefully gripping a ruffle of leaves.

SCHLOPP!

She pulled a dark green vegetable out of the mud and held it at arm's length. 'Dev, do you know what this is?'

It looked to Dev a bit like a hibbicus plant. Back in Eden, the adults grew and fermented hibbicus plants to make *hibbicus beer*, a particularly fiery drink known for its strong, bitter taste, and its habit of catching fire in the glass.

But this hibbicus looked different.

Dev reached out to touch its brittle, withered skin. An oily black dew smeared between his fingers. 'It's a hibbicus,' he said. 'But they're usually fat and green, with bright green leaves. This one—'

'This one is rotten,' Keeper interrupted. '*All* the hibbicus in Darkwater are rotten. And the rotten ones are even more *explosive* than usual.'

'HIBB-KISS!' Boja proclaimed, grabbing the hibbicus plant before Keeper could stop him. A crackle of flember sparkled out between his paws, plumpening the tired, blackened hibbicus and ripening it to its full freshness.

He brought it closer to his wide-open mouth. His eyes closed. His tongue waggled in anticipation.

'NO!' Keeper yelled, grabbing the hibbicus back. As she pulled it away, a mist of flember flowed out through its skin, wafting across the air and back into Boja's fingers. The hibbicus started to rot and wither in her hands. She stared at it in disbelief. 'What . . . what did you *do*?'

'Boja can share his flember,' Dev smiled proudly. 'I think it's to do with the flemberthyst crystal he bit into when he was born. He can ripen anything that grows with it, and if he eats that food then, well, he's just taking his own flember back in.'

Keeper puffed out her cheeks. 'Well that could be useful around here . . .' she started, before Boja yoinked the hibbicus from her hands, sparkled it full of flember and plumpened it once again. 'Like the bobbly-berry.' He grinned, once again lifting it towards his mouth. Keeper reached to snatch it back, her metal fingers sinking into its husk. Flames sparked out. She shrieked, yanking the hibbicus away from Boja's paws, away from his flember, as she flung it high into the air and quickly huddled over Dev.

With a loud BOOM the hibbicus exploded above them.

A shower of rusted debris clattered down.

'I told you the hibbicus here are HIGHLY explosive.'

Keeper coughed. She scraped a lump of smoking hibbi-cus off her shoulder. 'They're good for blowing holes in things. They're not so good for eating. You, bear, do you understand what I'm *saying*?'

A sizeable chunk of rusted engine CLONKED onto Boja's head.

'Hungry.' He pouted.

Then, just as quickly, Boja's mood changed again. His bottom lip dropped. His eyes bulged. He stared excitedly down to the ring below them, gesturing wildly towards something rustling through the wreckage.

'FEVVUS!' he shrieked. 'FEVVUS CAME WITH US!'

9
Not Fervus

A goat stood below them, its pale skin stretched taut across its long, bony face. A couple of yellow teeth stuck out from its mouth. Its hair was dark, grey, matted thick in some patches, and scraped off in others. Its wobbly legs seemed barely able to hold its little body up.

'BEHHHH!' it warned angrily.

'FEVVUS!' Boja squealed back.

'Boja, I don't think that's Fervus,' Dev warned. 'It looks more like a . . . *mean* Fervus.'

Boja didn't hear a word of it. He was already flinging himself over the wreckage and tumbling down to the ring below. He crashed, bum first, through the roof of a shed, then rolled out through its doors. Before Dev could shout 'please don't chase that goat', Boja was chasing the goat. His arms outstretched. His tongue flapping in the wind.

A look of sheer delight on his face.

Mean Fervus BEHHHHH-d in alarm, scooting between a pile of crumpled mine carts. Boja barrelled through them with his stomach. 'FEVVVVUS!' He roared with laughter. 'FEVVVVUS, COME BACK!'

'That . . .' Keeper spluttered with rage. 'That . . . BEAR!'

'Sorry, Keeper! I'll get him back!'

'BE CAREFUL OF THE HIBBICUS!' Keeper yelled. But Dev was already gone, sliding down to the ring below, following Boja's trail of destruction through the snarls, bleats, growls, giggles and honks that echoed around the quarry.

'BOJA!' Dev shouted. 'Boja, slow down!'

'BUT IT'S FEVVUS!' Boja beamed, as he clambered up the side of a rusted old crane.

'It's not Fervus. Fervus is in Eden. We're not IN Eden any more!'

Dev stumbled over a pipe, falling just short of a clump of hibbicus leaves. Holding his breath, he backed away slowly, only for his hand to brush against another clump. 'This is like a minefield!'

A loud creaking sound suddenly tore across the quarry. Boja, it seemed, was far too heavy for the crane he was perched upon, and it was buckling under his weight. 'WEEE-AAAAA-WOOOOO!' he cheered, riding the crane down towards the ground before disappearing into a huge plume of dust. And then – BOOM! An almighty explosion flung Boja back into sight, spinning him around in the air as he grinned inanely at Dev.

'Found . . . HIBB-KISS,' he garbled, tumbling back down into the shadows of the quarry. Dev raced towards him, sliding down into the next ring, hopping frantically around the hibbicus leaves as he called out for Boja.

But by the time he got there, Boja had already gone.

'BEHHH!' Mean Fervus bleated from somewhere

deeper down inside the quarry.

'BEHHHHHHH!' Boja boomed back.

Dev followed their voices down into the lowest ring, but he was starting to feel tired. Rebecca was right. The journey from Eden – or rather, the *roll* from Eden – had clearly weakened him. He slowed to catch his breath. His hand stretched out, feeling his way around the dark rocky cavern

He'd taken a wrong turn somewhere.

Walked into a dead end.

He felt leaves under his fingers. Withered, crinkled leaves.

More hibbicus plants.

And they were *everywhere.*

His heart pounded loudly in his ears.

'Oh, flip,' he whispered, unsure which way to turn.

'Oh, flip, oh flip, oh—'

'BEHHHH!'

Dev turned to see Mean Fervus blur past, then a huge red giggling bear, both of them racing towards the quarry's central column of rock. Mean Fervus leapt up onto its scaffolding, leaping from platform to platform. Then STOMP! STOMP! CLATTER! STOMP! Boja followed behind, excitedly jumping as if he and the little goat weighed the same.

'Boja, be CAREFUL!' Dev yelled, wincing as the platforms creaked noisily under the bear's heavy feet. He cautiously backed away from the hibbicus leaves and started to follow, clinging onto the bent-pipe railings as he climbed the platforms higher and higher and higher out of the quarry.

Back into the drizzle.

And up to the very top.

He staggered into the low light of early evening, towards the huge domed building. It was as wide as it was tall, its walls pitted with half-collapsed archways all painted black with a thick, tarry goop. Pylons surrounded its perimeter, their long, rattling chains trailing in through what was left of its roof. And on its front hung a sign. A rusted, battered sign, with a face Dev had seen before.

'HEY, DEV!' Boja and Mean Fervus were having a stand-off inside the building's main archway. Mean Fervus growled protectively. Boja grinned and waved. 'ME AND FEVVVUS ARE PLAYING!'

Dev made his way towards them, but he was struggling. His head was swimming. His lungs felt like they might burst. He knelt down, trying to catch a breath while his eyes started to focus again.

And then he saw something glinting in the dirt.

He crawled closer, reached out a hand, and slid a small, hard stone out from between where Boja and Mean Fervus were standing As he brought it up to the early evening light he could see myriad colours glistening inside.

'Is it FOOD?' Boja asked hopefully.

'It's better than that.' Dev's voice trembled. 'It's a . . . *flemberthyst crystal.*'

10
A Way In

'ARE YOU BOTH CRAZY?' Keeper clanked up the precarious spiral of metal platforms. 'THIS QUARRY IS LITTERED WITH HIBBICUS! ANY ONE OF THEM COULD HAVE BLOWN YOU UP!'

Once she reached the top, her whole body heaved with a loud hiss of steam. 'Dev, this is NOT the place to go exploring.' She sighed.

'Keeper, LOOK!' Dev cried, holding the crystal out between his finger and thumb. 'I found a flemberthyst!'

Keeper peered at it closely. 'So you did.'

'You wait until you see it *glowing*!' Dev replied. 'I saw loads of flemberthysts inside a cave in Eden – my Nonna showed them to me. The Flember Stream travelled up through them, all the way to the surface, and lit them all up like a million light bulbs!' He leapt excitedly on the spot. 'If we've found a flemberthyst, then we might be near to the Flember Stream!'

'I told you already,' Keeper huffed. 'There's no flember left in Darkwater.'

'The Flember Stream's here, the map says it is.' Dev clenched his fist around the flemberthyst. 'So where did all Darkwater's flember go? And why is there a flemberthyst all the way up here on the surface?'

He stared up at the big, fluffy-cheeked face on the sign above him.

Wilburforce Mining Corp.

Mining Corp.

MINING!

'You said you were mining shiny rocks. You were talking about *flemberthysts!*' Dev shrieked. 'That guy with the crazy hair, I saw him in the painting, and now up THERE too! He was in charge, right? He mined all the flemberthysts out of the ground, didn't he, and now there's no way for flember to reach the surface!'

Keeper spoke in a low voice. 'Wilburforce, he—'

'He's not here, I know. Rebecca told me. But if Albert Wilburforce was digging up flemberthysts, then maybe his mines lead right down to the Flember Stream! If we could just get down there I bet we could find it. We could find a way to bring flember back to Darkwater, and then me and Boja could carry some home for the Eden Tree! We could fix *everything!*'

Dev hopped between Boja and Mean Fervus, moving towards two large metal doors inside the archway. 'We just need to find a way in,' he mused, feeling around for a lock, or a bolt, or anything he might be able to undo. But there was nothing. Nothing except a small metal box clamped to the wall, with a red light flashing above it.

'Blessed be Dahlia,' Dev muttered under his breath. 'Who's *Dahlia?*'

A pair of metal arms locked around his chest, hauling him up off the ground. 'We should go,' Keeper growled. 'It's getting dark.'

'Not yet!' Dev pleaded. 'I want to look inside the mines!'

'You can go looking for rocks another time.'

'They're called *flemberthysts!*'

'I KNOW WHAT THEY'RE CALLED.'

An awkward silence filled the air, a silence only broken by raindrops TINK-TINK-TINK-TONK-ing across Keeper's shoulders.

Mean Fervus took his chance. He broke away from Boja and leapt, yellow teeth bared, he chomped

89

the crystal from Dev's hand. Then he turned, skidded between Boja's legs, and within seconds Mean Fervus disappeared beneath a pile of upturned mine carts.

'The flemberthyst!' Dev yelled.

'Leave it!' Keeper snapped, carrying Dev away from the doors. 'If we don't leave now we'll be walking back to the Village at night. And Darkwater is no place to be stomping around in the dark, not unless you want to tread on a hibbicus and blow yourself into the sky.'

Dev grimaced at the memory of Boja being flung around by an exploding hibbicus. 'OK, OK.' He sighed. 'But can we come back here tomorrow?'

'Maybe,' Keeper replied.

'Maybe!' Dev grinned, an excited cheer inside his chest. If Keeper was anything like his mum, a maybe could become a yes with just a little more persistence.

And a *yes* could bring them even closer to the Flember Stream.

11
Stew

Back inside the Village it was as warm as a fart, and just as unpleasant-smelling. The air hung thick and muggy, hazing around the glowing green lanterns that swayed gently from the ceiling. All the miners of Darkwater were in here. They looked old and tired. Their faces were craggy, scarred or drooping, their hair either wild or missing completely. Some wore dark goggles, while others hid behind scarves, hoods or over-sized beards. Their overalls were dirty, their boots were heavy. Everything clinked, rustled or growled as they moved.

That is until they saw Boja, squeezing himself in through the double doors, and everyone fell silent.

Everyone except Rebecca.

'THERE you all are!' She stretched her arms out wide. 'You've been gone so long!'

Keeper perched Dev onto the bar as if he were an ornament. 'Keep him here, OK? And the bear. I don't want to spend the night chasing after them both.'

'Won't you stay too, Keeper?' Rebecca asked. 'Have something to eat with us here, in the warm. Can't be very cosy in that cold tower of yours.'

'Tower?' Dev peeped.

Keeper rolled her eyes. 'I have a busy night,' she huffed, dragging her shawls across the Village and out through the double doors. 'I *always* have a busy night.'

Dev turned to Rebecca. 'Keeper has a *tower?*'

'Sounds grander than it is,' Rebecca replied. 'But you two are just in time. I was about to prepare dinner!'

Dinner! Both Dev and Boja's stomachs rumbled at the thought of it. Boja's rumbled so loud it shook the whole Village, rattling the pictures on the walls.

'I'll make sure *you* get double helpings,' Rebecca squeaked, spinning open a hatch behind the bar, pulling on a pair of long, rubber gloves and lowering herself down into the storeroom.

Dev turned to Boja and started checking him over. The big red bear had, after all, tumbled down into the quarry and been exploded into the air by a hibbicus plant, and yet all he had to show for it was a charred patch of fur on his bottom. 'Are you OK?' he asked, poking a finger into Boja's ear. 'No aches? No pains? That was quite an explosion.'

'Hibb-kiss!' Boja giggled, clearly having enjoyed the experience much more than Dev had enjoyed watching it.

Suddenly Rebecca was back, hauling a crate of blackened, withered hibbicus up and onto the floor. She carried it carefully, ve-e-e-ry carefully, to the pipes against the wall, before tipping it over one of the funnels.

Suddenly the whole room was alive with noise. The hibbicus plants CLONK-ed and CLANG-ed and FUDD-UDD-ed their way up the maze of pipes, across the ceiling and into the fat end of the huge, metal stalactite. BOOM! BOOM! BOOM! Small explosions dented out from its sides. SKKKK! CLANK! WHIRRRR! Hibbicus rattled their way down inside it, and then SPLTHPTHPTH! Something rather disgusting-sounding worked its way through the thin nozzles at the end.

Rebecca raised a bowl. Then she pulled one of a multitude of dangling cords, and watched with delight as a swirl of sickeningly oily stew curled out.

'STEW'S UP!' she yelled, sliding the first bowl towards Dev. He looked down at the same mulch he'd been offered earlier. Black and green and weirdly lumpy. His stomach turned at the sight of it. The miners didn't look too excited either, each of them grabbing at their bowls, whispering, 'Dahlia save us,' then reluctantly shovelling the oily muck into their mouths. They burped, one after the other, before clutching their stomachs in pain.

'If you don't like stew, Dev, then you're clean out of luck.' Rebecca slapped the hulking great contraption hanging down beside her. 'This clever machine right here is the HIBBICANNON, and it keeps all of Darkwater fed. We can get a whole load of delicious meals out of it. Stew, for one thing. Then there's stew soup, stew casserole, cold stew, stew cake, lumps of old stew on a stick, stew stew, and leftover stew.'

She yanked on a different cord. The machine spat a disgusting lump of brown into a mug, followed by a trickle of steaming liquid. 'Maybe a drink of lukewarm stew smoothie, instead?'

Dev's cheeks flushed a pale shade of green.

Rebecca shrugged, and took a gulp herself. 'To WILBURFORCE!' she shouted, swinging the mug up towards the painting of Albert Wilburforce.

All the other miners joined the toast, raising their bowls and spilling most of their stew down themselves.

With one more, huge gulp, Rebecca downed her brown sludge, and unleashed an extraordinarily loud belch.

'There's quite a fire in it.' She winced, steadying herself against the bar. 'You're getting all of the hibbicus plant in there, including the explosions.' She held her chest, gurning as if she'd just swallowed a pile of rocks.

Dev stared back at her in horror. Then he turned to Boja, who was lifting a bowl of stew up to his mouth and licking his lips excitedly.

'Maybe let's not eat the stew,' Dev whispered, grabbing the bowl from Boja's paws. 'It's making everyone look unwell. I still have vegetables in my pocket, the ones I picked from the Wildening, so we can share them later instead. They're old and withered but they'd be tasty for you when you fill them with your flember.'

Boja watched his bowl being passed along the bar to someone else. His bottom lip trembled as he tried to hold back the tears.

Suddenly everyone in the Village started cheering. A short, squat man, his greying blond hair pulled so far back into a bun that it stretched his face around his head, had climbed up onto one of the tables. He had no eyebrows, at least not until he raised a hand and drew, with his blackened fingers, two arched lines over his forehead.

He cleared his throat.

'Go on, Nobbins!' someone called out.

'Ohhhhhh . . .' the man on the table started, in a key clearly too high for his range.

'What blessed souls are we—'

Burp!

'Eating hibbicus by the sea—'

Burp! Burp!

'What delicious stew . . .'

He gulped, as if holding back sick.

'We chew . . . chew . . . chew—'

Bu-u-urp!

'No happier could . . . we . . . *be-e-e-O-O-U-U-U-U-U-RP!*'

The song was sung again, this time with the accompaniment of all the other miners. They mumbled, groaned and burped the words to their own, lazy tunes, then everyone raised their stews towards the painting, and toasted Wilburforce again.

'PRIEST!' someone suddenly yelled from one of the windows. 'Priest is coming!'

Chairs scraped noisily across the floor. A few of the older miners disappeared into their tents. Nobbins tumbled from his table and scrambled to the double doors. A woman – tall, hunched, her own hair tucked beneath a buckled hat – ran to the other side.

'Don't look him in the eye, dear Elise.' Nobbins stared at the floor.

'I *know*,' Elise spat back.

They waited, in deathly silence.

Until . . .

Scuttle.

Scuttle scuttle.

It came from beneath them. An unsettling sound, like that of someone, or something, crawling around outside. A few clonks along the gangway. A few more, towards the door.

CLONK.

CLONK CLONK.

Nobbins reached his trembling hand towards the handle, preparing to let whatever it was inside.

A coldness seemed to descend upon the Village.

And a shiver ran through Dev's bones.

12
Priest

'P . . . P . . . Priest.' Nobbins and Elise creaked the doors open. 'To what do we owe this – *burp* – p . . . p . . . pleasure?'

A tall figure climbed in, all joints and elbows, like a gopplespider crawling out from behind a cupboard. Dev couldn't tell which were limbs and which were shadows as both unfolded across the floor. A long, hooded black cloak, still glistening from the rain, concealed most of the face beneath it.

But Dev could still see what was hanging around the figure's neck.

Flemberthyst crystals.

And they were *glowing*.

'The bear,' a low voice drawled. 'I want to see the bear.'

A thin, withered arm stretched out from inside the cloak and shakily pushed the hood away. The face below was as white as a ghost. It looked uneven, mangled, as if half of it was missing.

Priest had only one eye. It was cloudy, watering, and it peered out across the room. Upon seeing Boja, Priest scurried forwards in a flurry of robes, his terrifying face drawing up close to Boja's shiny black nose.

'Hello.' Boja smiled.

'There it issss . . .' Priest hissed, a glistening trail of spittle escaping from his jagged black teeth and trickling down his pointed chin. 'And what a *fine* monster you are.'

Boja's face scrunched up, and he snorted in disgust. 'Not a monster.'

'*Not* a monster, of course.' Priest squeezed Boja's belly between his pointed fingers. 'But big. And fat. And strong. *Full* of flember, I'd bet.'

Boja's grumpy face started to soften. And a giggle escaped his lips.

'B . . . Boja's my *friend*,' Dev stammered, reaching to pull Priest's hand away but suddenly feeling woozy. He wasn't sure if it was the lasting effects of falling down a mountain, or Priest's stale, salty breath, but something was making his head swim again.

'Your . . . *friend?*' Priest let go of Boja's belly. 'Well, we are very, *very* grateful you brought your friend down to meet us.'

Dev glanced at the nametag on Priest's robes.

'They just call me Priest,' he whispered, patting a stool

HELMUT J. PRIEST
—RESOURCE DISTRIBUTION—
WILBURFORCE MINING CORPORATION

for Dev to sit on. 'Tell me, lad . . . how long have you been in Darkwater?'

'Not long,' Dev replied. 'Not even a day.'

Priest brushed up close against him. 'Have you seen . . . the *sea*?'

The closer he leant in, the woozier Dev felt.

'N . . . no,' Dev replied.

'Good,' Priest whispered. 'Gooood. You stay up here, in the Village, where it's safe.'

He paused, pulling his hand back to wipe a little more spittle from his chin. 'And while you're both here, enjoy Darkwater's . . . *hospitality.*' Priest grabbed an untouched bowl of stew and slid it along the bar, right in front of Boja's nose. Before Dev could even say a word, Boja had flung the whole thing, metal bowl and all, into his wide-open mouth.

'Mmf . . . mmf . . . mmf . . .' He beamed, chomping and crunching in sheer delight. 'DESHISCHUS!'

Then Boja grabbed another bowl and crumpled it into his mouth too.

And another.

And another.

'Boja, slow down!' Dev cried, but there was no stopping him now. Boja had the scent of food, his nose pulling him to each and every table as he picked up all the half-finished bowls of stew and wolfed them down.

And then Boja was *dancing*. Arms out, flapping like an alarmed goose and mumbling Nobbins's song about stew (the words to which he only vaguely remembered). And then he was spinning. And spinning. And spinning so fast he became dizzy, before crashing loudly through a stack of tables.

'WHSCH DEDGEISHUS SCHOOOO!' he cheered, plucking great chunks of stew from his belly fur and slurping them into his mouth.

Elise kicked at Boja's waggling feet. 'Stop – burp! – EATING all our STEW.'

Nobbins hurriedly wiped the startled eyebrows from his forehead and redrew them scrunched down into a scowl. 'It's all we have to – burp! – EAT!'

More would have raised their voices, had not a noise rumbled from deep inside Boja's tummy. A noise so strange, so unsettling, it made everyone take a step back.

B-O-I-L-K-K-K!

Boja's smile vanished. He sat alert, his blackened lips wobbling in fear. His eyes widened in panic.

'Boja?' Dev squeezed through the miners and edged

towards the bear. 'Boja, are you OK?'

B-O-I-L-L-L-K-K-K-K-K-K-K-K-K-K!

Dev gulped nervously.

Boja was clearly *not* OK.

13
Stinkflame

Boja staggered to his feet. His big red stomach BOILK-ed and FIZZ-ed and GNURGGGGGLE-ed like a volcano ready to explode.

'Dev!' he whimpered. 'DEVVVVV!'

'It's OK. Boja, it's—'

'Urp!'

Boja's tiny little burp surprised them both. As did the waft of grey smoke which followed out from his mouth.

'Urp!' he went again.

'Urp! Urp! Urp!'

'Stew gives us *all* the burps,' Rebecca laughed, peeping out from behind the bar. 'That's the hibbicus. It's quite normal.'

'BU-U-U-U--URPPPPPPP!' Boja suddenly boomed, a powerful blast of flame exploding out from his mouth and propelling him back against the wall.

'BU-U-U-U-U-U-RPPPPPPPP!' he repeated, belching fire above the heads of the crowd. It caught on their hats and ignited whatever stray hairs they had left.

'That's NOT NORMAL!' Priest shouted.

'BU-U-U-U-U-U-U-U-U-U-U-RRRPPPP! BURP! BURP BURP!' Blast after blast of bright yellow flames spilled out from Boja's mouth, catching the wallpaper, the pictures, the long, flowing curtains.

'Our VILLAGE!' Rebecca yelped, frantically slamming the flames with the remains of someone's tent. 'He's destroying it!'

Dev grabbed an empty stew bowl, holding it up as a shield. 'Boja, go outside!' he shouted. 'Out through the doors, just until this passes!'

Boja tried, but he was too disorientated by the thick black smoke now rolling through the Village and he only managed to crash into the wall. It looked like another burp was building inside of him. He put his paws over his mouth to hold it in, only for his cheeks to balloon out as a huge fiery HICC-URP

somersaulted him backwards over the bar.

Dev raced to help, but Boja was already up and away, stomping madly around the Village. He gibbered and shrieked, his arms waving, desperate to find a door, a window, any route out of there.

And then he saw the hibbicannon.

He leapt onto it, clawing his way to the top as if he were climbing a tree. It CRE-E-E-EAK-ed under his weight, then WR-E-E-ENCH-ed away from its pipes, its end nozzles rising up into the air and firing a splodge of stew across the Village. As Boja scrambled from one end of the hibbicannon to the other it swung upon its supports, oily goo splattering out across the tents, catching into flames before exploding into huge fires.

Dev threw down his shield, ran up the stairs to the second-floor balcony, climbed over the railing and waited for the thin end of the hibbicannon to swing underneath him. Then he flung himself out towards it. He landed with a CLANG, struggling to grip on as he was swung high above the Village.

'It's OK!' Dev shouted, slowly climbing towards the terrified bear. 'Boja, it's OK. I think you've stopped burping.'

Boja wobbled to his feet as he tried to stand upon the hibbicannon's wider end, and stared straight back at Dev. He had fear in his eyes. 'Sohh-rry,' he gulped, clutching his buttocks in panic before the loudest, most ground-shaking fart Dev had ever heard blasted out from between them.

FFFR-R-R-R-R-R-R-R-R-R-R-RPPPPP!

It rocketed Boja forwards upon a billowing black flame, along the full length of the hibbicannon and off the other end. He slammed face first into the wall or, more specifically, right through the painting of Albert Wilburforce hanging upon it.

His huge, furry bottom dangled high above them all.

The whole Village started to creak slowly under his weight. Suddenly the hibbicannon broke free of its supports and slammed down to the floor, tilting everything back the other way.

The lanterns flickered. The dust settled.

A hush fell.

'Boja,' Dev whispered to the huge red bear embedded in the painting. 'Boja, are you OK?'

Boja's bottom heaved. One last little puff of smoke FRRP-ed out from between his buttocks. Then Dev heard a gentle snore coming from the other side of the wall.

'I was right, there's a whole LOT of flember in that monster!' Priest wailed with delight.

Rebecca's head poked out from what was left of the bar. She stared at the remains of the Village, the burnt walls, the buckled floor, all the smashed and crumpled furniture. And a tear trickled down her pale cheek.

'That BEAR . . .' said Cled, as he angrily patted out the fire in his beard. 'That bear just broke our HIBBICANNON! Now what will we do for FOOD?'

'I . . . I can help,' Dev stammered. 'Maybe I can repair it. Yes! Let me *repair* the hibbicannon!'

'YOU?' Cled clenched his fists so tight his knuckles cracked. 'You're just a boy. What could *you* possibly know about a machine like this?'

'I *fix* things,' Dev replied with a nervous smile. 'It's what I do.'

14
The Hibbicannon

The first step was to figure out what the hibbicannon was, and how it worked. Dev climbed around it, sticking his head inside its broken parts and trying to see what made it tick. At his best guess it worked like some kind of huge oven. The larger end was heavily insulated;

this, presumably, was where the explosive hibbicus plants were mulched. This goop, or 'stew' as Rebecca insisted on calling it, could then be channelled through into different sections depending on what dish was being served. Concentrated into a paste, thinned into a sauce, or just FLUMP-ed out like the gross snot it was.

By the time Dev had an understanding of how it worked, a realization dawned upon him.

Why just fix the hibbicannon?

When he could *improve* it.

Dev squeezed through the crowd of miners and raced up the stairs. A few loud thuds later, and he was clomping back down, carrying all the broken tools he'd packed for his journey. They dropped to the floor with a thud, a clang, and a burst of sparks, which made everyone watching go 'oooh!'

'None of these things work any more,' he proudly announced, pulling the Ripplybollop, the Optylopops and the spring-loaded Fisplestaw apart. He laid them alongside the Fibbulator, the Bimcockle and the Rassleclock. 'But when you're an inventor, you work with what you've got!'

He stretched out his arms, rolled his head, and took a deep breath. 'And I, Dev P. Everdew, can work with *anything.*'

With an excited gurgle in his belly, Dev made a start. He reached into the hibbicannon and wrenched its insides out:, nobbles, flangules and strange twisty pipelets that didn't seem to do anything, so he threw them away. He figured he could replace most of them with soggy Optylopops anyway, screwing the Bimcockle in between them. The Fibbulator could double up as a junction box, the Rassleclock a timer, and the Ripplybollop perfectly replaced the hibbicannon's twisted nozzles. The spring-loaded Fisplestaw he just used to hammer it all together. It beeped and it sparked, but it seemed to do the job.

INVENTION 503: The Hibbicannon Mark Two

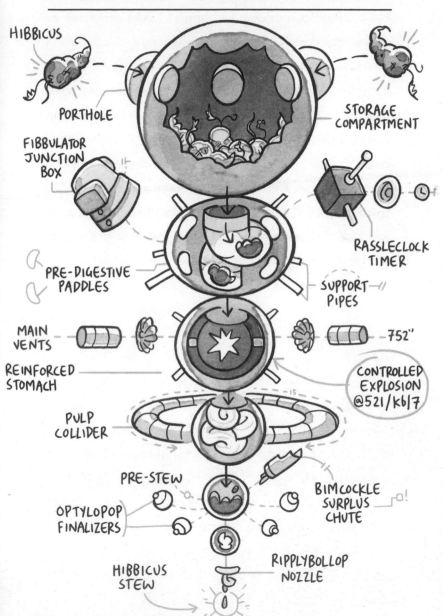

HIBBICUS

PORTHOLE

STORAGE COMPARTMENT

FIBBULATOR JUNCTION BOX

RASSLECLOCK TIMER

PRE-DIGESTIVE PADDLES

SUPPORT PIPES

MAIN VENTS

752"

REINFORCED STOMACH

CONTROLLED EXPLOSION @521/kb/7

PULP COLLIDER

PRE-STEW

BIMCOCKLE SURPLUS CHUTE

OPTYLOPOP FINALIZERS

HIBBICUS STEW

RIPPLYBOLLOP NOZZLE

'There!' Dev wiped a smear of grease across his fore-head. 'Now let me show you how it works.' He beamed at the crowd of hungry miners. 'Rebecca, can I have a hibbicus plant, please?'

Rebecca drew her eyes away from the machine, nodded, reached down inside her hatch and pulled up a withered black hibbicus. 'Be careful,' she whispered, handing it to Dev. 'They're not for playing around with.'

'Oh, I know.' Dev hopped to the far end of the hibbi-cannon, opened a small porthole, slid the hibbicus inside and closed it again. 'This compartment can store up to thirty-eight hibbicus plants at once,' he proclaimed. 'So you won't need to load it up too often!'

He slammed his fist against the side of the hibbi-cannon. It rumbled, it clanked and it groaned as the hibbicus plant started to noisily rattle its way through.

'I saw how much the stew made your stomachs hurt. You said it was because you were eating all the explosive power of the hibbicus, but that gave me an idea.' A flame blasted out from one of the pipes, along with a rather unpleasant BU-U-U-URPPP! Then another flame, and another BU-U-U-U-URPPP from a pipe on the other side. Soon, flames were burping out all along the hib-bicannon. 'I made it so the hibbicannon explodes the hibbicus for you. I designed it like Boja's stomach, so the explosions are released as flaming belches. Now your stew should be safe to eat!'

A swell of excitement rose through Dev's chest. He grabbed an empty stew bowl and held it beneath one of the thin nozzles.

'Who's first?' He grinned.

Nothing came out.

'I don't understand,' Dev muttered. 'I thought I'd—'

BANG! One of the Optylopops flew out from inside the hibbicannon, piercing the wall. BANG! BANG BANG! More of them, whizzing about like popcorn. The miners shrieked and ducked, scurrying for cover. The Bimcockle blasted out in a plume of smoke. The

Rassleclock exploded, the Fibbulator spun a hole through the floor, the Ripplybollop started to bulge like Boja's belly. And then – BOOM! – an almighty explosion burst out from underneath it all, flinging the hibbicannon up like a rocket.

It crashed through the ceiling, before disappearing into the night sky.

Dev stood beneath the new hole in the roof. He listened for the quiet CRUMP of a hibbicannon landing somewhere far in the distance, then he turned towards the wide-eyed miners.

'I . . . I'm not sure what went wrong . . .' he stuttered, the rain pattering down upon his head.

'I do.' Cled pulled an Optylopop out from the wall and flung it angrily to the ground. 'You and your bear came to DARKWATER!'

15
Day Two

After the hibbicannon's impromptu flight across Darkwater, Dev was tasked with going outside to fix the hole in the roof. He was glad to. Even though the night was cold, even though it was raining, it was still preferable to staying inside the Village with all the angry miners. At least out here maybe he could *fix* something properly.

He sighed, pulled his scarf over his nose, and followed the gangway round to where Boja's head was still wedged through the wall. His big bulging eyes were closed now. His mouth whistled out a snore.

Dev patted the bear reassuringly on the nose.

'You sleep it off.' He smiled.

Dev carefully climbed down one of the rope ladders, walked across the soggy mud, and set to work searching for stray bits of metal. There was plenty piled up against the quarry wall. He pulled out a few thick, flat pieces, and dragged them back towards the Village.

With no Boja to help him carry the metal back up to the roof, it took Dev a while, and using old bolts to nail them in place took even longer. But eventually the job was done, and once he was satisfied the Village would be dry for the night, Dev used any leftover scraps to build a small canopy over Boja's head. He snuggled in alongside the bear until he too was covered from the rain, resting his head into the dark, wet fur of Boja's cheek.

Dev's whole body ached. His mind, however, wasn't ready for sleep. It was far too busy wondering what might be happening back in Eden.

'We've been gone for ages,' he muttered. 'Mum will be worried.'

He felt a pang of guilt at the thought of it.

'Maybe she told Acting Mayor Bastor to take a Guild search party out beyond the Wall. And maybe he did. Maybe they're all making their way down the mountain right now. Maybe the Wildening is attacking them too!'

Dev shuddered, running his fingers across the black scratches on his arm. 'I hope they don't come.' He sighed. 'Even though I'd do anything to see someone from Eden again, I hope they all stay where they are. Where it's safe.'

Boja snorted. It was a sleepy, snotty snort, followed by the delicate squeak of a fart from his bum still stuck inside the Village. Dev could hear muffled voices through the wall – they were mostly, from what he could work out, complaining about the smell.

Boja giggled in his sleep.

'We'll just stay in Darkwater a little longer,' Dev said, fishing around in his pocket for the food he'd salvaged from the Wildening. He pulled out an old cauliflower, a spricket, a few small peppers and a couple of flonions.

None of them looked particularly edible.

'Keeper will take us into the mines, we'll find the Flember Stream, and then we'll take some flember home for the Eden Tree.' He nibbled on the flonion, and nuzzled closer into Boja's fur. 'And we'll do it all *together*.'

The next thing Dev knew, the skies had lightened into a bundle of delicate greys, the rain lessened to a drizzle.

He must have fallen asleep too.

'Boja . . .' he mumbled. 'Boja, wake up . . .'

He shrieked. What stuck out from the wall beside him was not the Boja he knew, but a far bigger, fluffier version of Boja. A night spent outside in the drizzle had fluffed Boja's head fur into a giant red pom-pom, his eyes, nose and mouth all buried somewhere inside it.

Dev flattened down what he could, combing Boja's fur with his hand, although he only ended up making him look even more ridiculous.

Boja was too asleep to notice.

Suddenly the front doors of the Village clanged

open. A gaggle of miners stepped out onto the gangway, stretching, yawning and scratching in the bleak morning light. Sleep had calmed them a little, but they were still grumbling about Dev. And Boja. And how they'd be going hungry tonight.

'Chance the sea might offer us better today,' old Grippins remarked, tugging his hat even further down upon his head.

'It hasn't bothered with us for weeks,' Nobbins replied. 'Probably forgotten we're here at all.'

'Ain't forgotten.' Elise clipped Nobbins's ear. 'You want to blame someone for us going hungry, you blame *Keeper*.'

They grunted in agreement.

'Well, whatever we find in the waters, may Dahlia bless us,' Nobbins said, swinging the rope ladder down the hatch.

'Dahlia bless us,' the others agreed as they each climbed down to the ground.

'Dahlia!' Dev whispered to himself. 'I know that name. I saw it written outside the mines.'

He crept out from the shadows, watching the miners as they disappeared into the murky drizzle.

'Maybe *Dahlia* can help us find the Flember Stream.' He smiled hopefully. 'Maybe *Dahlia* can help us go home!'

16
To the Coast

Boja grumbled, his eyelids slowly opening. 'Break-fascht,' he drawled through his big fluffy face.

'Not yet. Can you get yourself out of this wall first?'

Boja blinked, seemingly surprised to find himself wedged half inside the Village, half outside. He shuffled a little, his chubby body squeaking as he tried to squeeze through. Dev reached up to grip his black shiny nose and he pulled. 'HNNNNRGHHHHH!' They both strained, until Boja came not out of the wall, but *with* the wall, a ballerina skirt of crumpled, ripped metal still clamped around his waist.

And a destroyed portrait of Albert Wilburforce collapsing around his ankles.

Boja wriggled his metal skirt down onto the gangway. His body had been kept safe and warm inside, but since his head had been left out to the mercy of the fluff-inducing drizzle Dev couldn't help but laugh at the sight of him.

'Mmf,' Boja sniffed, idly scratching his belly with one paw, picking lumps of dried hibbicus stew from around his mouth with the other.

'It's fine, you look fine.' Dev chuckled, swinging down the rope ladder. 'Now hurry up! I don't want to lose sight of the miners!' He landed on the muddy ground with a squelch. Boja landed with more of a SPLUTCH, the noise of a bear who'd missed the first few rungs of the ladder and tumbled down the rest. He huffed and puffed as he pushed himself onto his feet, then trudged along behind Dev.

The two of them followed the miners from a distance, watching as they snaked over the edge of the cliff and then down the narrow path into the quarry, along the outer ring. Dev was keen to stay out of sight, ducking behind wreckage whenever he thought they might be spotted. Boja, however, was far more concerned about the hibbicus leaves sprouting around them. He clutched his tummy, and then his bottom, and groaned at the memory of what those withered old plants had done to him.

'No more . . . stew . . .' he whined.

'Here.' Dev pulled a small, tired-looking cauliflower from his pocket. 'Try one of these instead.'

Boja took the cauliflower between his fingers. A gentle crackle of flember passed across it and suddenly he was holding something far thicker and riper than the vegetable Dev had offered him.

He plopped it into his mouth, and began crunching contentedly.

'I don't think I'll ever get

tired of seeing you do that,' Dev laughed. Then he stared wistfully at his own, rather unappetizing, withered spricket. 'Shame I can't share my flember too.'

By the time they reached the craggy outer wall, the miners were already climbing the calamity of wooden planks and platforms embedded in it. Dev was quick to follow them. He could hear the roar of the sea beyond. He could feel its salty spray. He hopped excitedly from step to step, leaping up onto the glistening wet rocks at the top before stopping, stunned, to gaze out upon one of the most beautiful sights he could have imagined.

The *sea*.

It stretched as wide as his eyes could see. An ocean of waves – huge, *huge* waves, swirling and splitting and tearing themselves apart only to *smash* right back together. A great din filled his ears. The sharp spray lashed his skin. Every breath, every deep, deep breath, brought only bitter cold into his lungs.

It was everything he'd hoped it would be.

And it was so much more.

And yet, from high up on the mountain, Dev had always thought the seas were blue. It darkened nearer the coastline, but that, he had assumed, was just the shadow from the rocks, the coves that curled around it, the momentous, sharp spines of the reef rising out from its waters. This close, however, he could see it more clearly.

The water here was *black*.

What, he wondered, could all the miners be looking for in a sea like this?

'Come to ruin this for us too, have you?' Nobbins glared up at Dev from one of the many wooden jetties hanging out from the rocks. 'Brought your bear? Maybe he can fart so hard it pushes one of us into the water?'

'N . . . no,' Dev stammered, just as Boja's sweaty, fluffy, bulbous head rose up behind him.

Elise was the first to laugh. She pointed a finger up at Boja, alerting the other miners to his huge, ridiculous

head, and soon they were all rolling about in hysterics.

Boja had absolutely no idea what they were laughing at. So he laughed along too, to be polite.

Dev started climbing down the rickety ladders. 'Dahlia,' he said. 'You all mentioned Dahlia, back at the Village. I saw her name by the mines too.'

The laughter stopped. '*Blessed* Dahlia,' Nobbins muttered, pulling out his blackened finger and drawing a large heart onto his chest. 'You don't say that name, boy. You ain't worthy to even hold it on your tongue.'

'Who . . . who *is* she?'

'Dahlia is the Foodbringer,' Elise replied. 'When she sees fit, we eat more than just filthy rotten hibbicus stew.' A happier memory flickered across her face. 'When Dahlia blesses us, we eat like *royalty*.'

'But she won't feed us nothing if we don't pay her,' Nobbins fussed, wrapping a length of chain around his arm. The other end had already been tied around an oil drum, which he kicked into the foaming water. 'And we can't pay her if nothing washes up. So if you wouldn't mind, lad, you're getting in our way.' He scowled. Dev took a few steps back. 'Pay her?'

Grippins appeared behind him. '*Gold*,' he hissed from beneath his floppy hat. 'Why, you got any on you?'

Prickles appeared on his other side. 'Clamp his jaw open! I'm telling you, he'll have some in his teeth!'

'I . . . I haven't got any gold,' Dev stuttered. He swallowed nervously as he thought of the beautiful gold heart thumping in Boja's chest, the gold heart he had placed there himself. 'But if I could help you find some, some gold for Dahlia, in return would you help us get inside the mines?'

'You want . . . to enter the SANCTUARY?' Prickles shrieked.

Nobbins swung around, slapping his dirty fingers across his damp forehead and drawing on two rather fierce eyebrows. 'You stay AWAY from the Sanctuary, lad. That's where Dahlia LIVES. You stay away from her, you stay AWAY from our Foodbringer.'

Elise grabbed the back of Dev's scarf and hoiked him backwards. 'Anyway,' she smirked, dragging him across the jetty. 'You won't find any gold before we do. Not unless you're going to dive into the sea for it.'

'And you might not want to do that.' Nobbins lifted his oil drum out from the water, its metal sides now bubbling and dissolving before Dev's eyes. 'Gold's the *only* thing the sea don't eat.'

17
Along the Coast

Dev climbed the ladders back to the higher line of rocks, then sat down next to Boja and his huge head.

Together they stared out across the black, rolling seas.

'They said she lives inside the mines,' Dev muttered. 'Dahlia – they said she lives down there. That's why they won't let us in. But if someone *does* live down there, then there must still be flember down there with them. And if there *is* flember, then it could lead us straight to the Flember Stream! Boja, we HAVE to get inside those mines.'

'You found the sea, then,' Priest hissed in Dev's ear.

'NYARGH!' Dev's heart jumped inside his chest.

'YARGHHHH!' Boja bellowed.

'My apologies. I didn't mean to . . . sssscare you,' Priest smirked, as his long, spindly limbs pulled the rest of his body down between them. He took a deep intake of breath and savoured the salty air. 'Isn't it . . . majestic?'

'It's black.' Dev tried to shuffle away. 'The water, it's as black as ink.'

'It is *boundless*,' Priest exhaled. 'Just like the night sky itself.'

'I saw Nobbins put an oil drum in the water,' Dev said. 'It came out full of holes! He said the sea *ate* it. That it eats everything except gold!'

Priest's eye glinted. 'I did warn you to stay away.' He

wrapped a robed arm around Dev's shoulders. 'We don't want you or your . . . *friend* . . . to be falling beneath the waves, do we?'

Dev started to feel woozy again. He gazed at the glowing crystals clinking around Priest's neck. 'Your . . . your flemberthysts,' he mumbled. 'Where did you find them?'

Priest looked down to his necklace. Then, with a loud heave and the pop-pop-pop of cracking bones, he unfolded his limbs and stood back up. 'I have more,' he said. 'Come away from the water, and I'll show you.'

Before Dev could even reply, Priest had started dragging his robes across the rocks of the coastline, his spindly shadow shuffling along towards a tall cove of sharpened rocks. Then he reached up, and started to climb. One crag to the next, to the next, hauling his ghoulish, black body up inside a hollow.

A hollow so dark and so scary-looking it made Dev's stomach bubble.

'I'm not keen on following him up there,' Dev said to Boja, nervously tugging his boots up. 'But if Priest has more flemberthysts, then maybe *he* knows how to get us into the mines. Anything which brings us closer to the Flember Stream, which will bring us *home*, has to be worth the risk.'

From somewhere inside the fluff, Boja whimpered.

'We'll be quick,' Dev insisted. 'I promise.'

He pulled Boja upright, and together they edged along the coastline between Darkwater and the sea. With the incessant drizzle, and now the spray from the waves, the rest of Boja's fur was floofing up too. Walking was quite difficult, so much so that Dev was rather concerned his big, floofy friend might tread a big, floofy foot too close to the rocky edge, and then tumble down into the sea.

As they neared the hollow, the rocks became even more difficult. They jutted out from the ground like a cavalcade of jagged, twisting spears, almost impossible to walk through were it not for Boja's excessively floofy feet. He sque-e-e-ezed his body between the spikes, picked up Dev and carried him in his arms like he was a precious new-born waffle.

'Boja, lift me higher!'

Boja gripped both paws around Dev's waist and hauled him up as high as he could reach. Dev scrambled onto a ledge of flatter ground, pulling himself up in front of the wide-open mouth of the hollow.

Boja whimpered again, as if it might make Dev change his mind and turn round.

'Just wait for me out here.' Dev smiled. 'I'll be back before you know it.'

Then he stepped into the darkness, and disappeared completely.

18
The Hollow

It felt deathly cold inside the hollow.

A panic slithered through Dev's bones.

'Priest?' His voice echoed out around him. 'Priest, are you in here?'

His eyes caught sight of something glowing in the darkness. It was a faint light, but it was *moving*, wisping between a few loose lumps of crystal lying on the ground.

'Flember.' Dev gasped. 'And . . . *flemberthysts!*'

These flemberthysts, however, didn't look like the ones Ventillo had shown him in Eden's caves. They didn't shine with the same brilliant white light. No, these crystals murmured. They struggled. They lit for a few seconds with the weakest of lights, and then they were dark again.

'I told you there were more.' A towering shadow flickered against the wall. Dev froze, watching in horror as Priest's long, scarred face emerged out from the darkness, his sharpened teeth grimacing into a smile.

'Flember . . .' Dev struggled to croak out the words. 'There . . . there *is* flember in Darkwater after all!'

Priest cast his beady eye over the crystals. 'Oh, no no no, this is *my* flember you see before you.' He grinned, picking one up and proudly stroking the light out from inside it. 'Every drop of it leaving my body, flowing through these little rocks and then back again.'

Dev stared at him in disbelief. 'That . . . that's not possible! Flember can't just leave someone's body like that, not unless they're Boja!'

'Sit among these crystals long enough and they start dra-w-w-wing it out of you.' Priest took a deep, satisfied breath. The glow inside each flemberthyst breathed with him. 'It takes a while. Hours. Days. Weeks. Months. These ones have been sucking out my flember for *years*. Then they pass it around, you see? One crystal . . . to the next . . . to the next, all the way back to me.' He scuttled behind Dev and clutched his shoulders. 'Isn't it beautiful to watch?' Priest whispered.

'I didn't know flemberthysts could pull your flember out.' Dev gasped. 'And then conduct it, like this, like electricity flowing around a *circuit* . . .'

Suddenly Priest slipped his fingers into Dev's backpack and pulled out a small glowing chunk of flemberthyst. 'They can pull *your* flember out too, lad. I hid this piece on you when we first met,' he hissed. 'You've been charging it up ever since.'

A weakness washed through Dev's limbs. He stared at the glowing crystal in amazement. 'That . . . that's stolen a bit of *my* flember?'

'A tiny amount.' Priest grinned. 'I hide a crystal on

everyone in Darkwater, taking a little bit of flember from each. Then, when I gets my chance, I give that flember away.'

'Away?'

'To the SEA.'

Suddenly Priest thrust the flemberthyst out in front of him and dropped it into a shallow puddle of water. A thick crack splintered across the crystal's surface, a crack which then shattered it into a hundred shards. Its glow dimmed, the water bubbled, and within seconds the flemberthyst had dissolved away beneath the surface.

Dev couldn't quite believe what he'd just seen. His mouth flapped open, trying to form words, but only making noises.

'Oh, don't take it so personally. I give my own flember too!' Priest lashed his foot out and kicked a stack of faintly glowing flemberthysts into the puddle. They too hissed loudly, cracking into shards before dissolving. 'The black waters *hunger*, lad. They demand *flember*! Better I give them a little here and there or the sea will wash right into Darkwater to eat *us* instead.'

He loomed in close.

'Don't you see? I take flember to HELP us all. I'm trying to keep us all SAFE.'

Every inch of Dev's skin prickled with fear. He threw himself down to the ground, grabbing an armful of crystals. 'Flemberthysts belong underground,' he shouted. 'Not up here. They're not for you to use to . . . to steal other people's flember!'

'We dug all the crystals up.' Priest shrugged. 'I've just been picking up the leftovers. You . . . do know that's my flember you're taking?'

The flemberthysts in Dev's arms started to fade. Flember wafted out, sparkling across the darkness, slipping back towards Priest and then sinking inside his robes. 'What did you call it? A circuit?' Priest chuckled.

'Yessss, I like that word. It's a *circuit*. Flember always flows back to where it belongs, back to its warm, host body. That's why I have to be so quick throwing these pretty little crystals into the water, or else they'd lose all that delicious flember.'

Dev tried not to listen. He didn't want anything more to do with Priest, didn't want to be anywhere near him. All he could think about was getting out of here and back to Boja. Then he'd be safe. Then he could work out what to do next.

'That's it, hold those crystals tight!' Priest called out. 'Fill them with the rest of your lovely flember.'

And then he laughed. A nasty, gurgling laugh, which echoed through the hollow and followed Dev all the way out into the daylight.

19
Scavengers

Thanks to Darkwater's relentless drizzle, what was once a Boja was now a huge, dripping fluffball, twice the size of the original. Still he gleefully raised his arms upon seeing Dev, lifted him down from the hollow and then squeezed them both through the spiky rocks.

Once on easier ground, Dev climbed out from Boja's paws.

'I grabbed all I could,' he said, clutching the heavy stack of flemberthysts. 'Boja, we need to get these crystals away from Priest before he can take anyone else's flember. We need to *hide* them.'

Boja reached out his big fluffy arms and scooped up the flemberthysts. 'Hide them.' He grinned.

'And QUICKLY,' Dev replied. 'Before they start taking our flember too!'

As they made their way back along the coast, the weather started to worsen. The drizzle became rain, the winds howled, and a thick, billowing mist started to roll across the waves. It had clearly been enough to drive the miners away from the water's edge, as Dev caught sight of Nobbins clambering up the wooden steps.

Nobbins, unfortunately, saw him too.

'What's that bear of yours carrying?' Nobbins sneered, his eyebrows dripping down his cheeks. 'Those rock things. Are they what we used to dig out of the ground?'

'They're prettier than I remember.' Elise pushed Nobbins with an ungracious shove to the face. Her eyes were transfixed on the flemberthysts. 'How does he make them glow like that?'

'GLOW?' Dev looked back. The flemberthysts in Boja's arms now shone with a bright, beautiful white light, the drizzle glinting as it swirled around them. 'Boja, they're drawing out your flember too quickly! Take it back! Take it back!'

'Hnnnngghhhh!' Boja strained to draw his flember back inside his body, but his fur was too thick. It muffled the flember, sending it crackling around his body like lightning across a storm cloud.

The flemberthysts only sparkled brighter.

Elise clasped her hands in glee. 'I can think of someone else who might find these glowing rocks pretty.'

'Dahlia . . .' Nobbins gasped.

Elise nodded. 'Why not? We spend all our time out here, dragging the seas for a few scraps of gold. And then this big fluffy bear comes along and brings us something even more beautiful.'

Nobbins wiped a palm across his forehead, blackening

it all into one big eyebrow. 'She would reward us well.'

'Boja, give me the crystals,' Dev shouted.

'No, no, give your *crystals* to me.' Elise held a hand out towards the terrified-looking bear.

Boja, unable to see anything, his eyes too far buried inside his big fluffy face, panicked. He tried to turn towards Dev, but his big floofy feet slipped upon the wet ground and sent him tumbling backwards. BONK BONK BONK! He rolled down one flight of steps, still clasping onto the flemberthysts. BONK BONK BONK! Down another, rolling along the jetty, his fall only halted by a cluster of oil drums that he sent splashing into the sea.

Where they then dissolved beneath the waves.

Elise was first after him. 'Give us those crystals!' she warned, picking up a length of pipe and swinging it over her shoulder. 'Give us the crystals, bear, or you're going into the sea!'

Dev scrambled down behind her, leapt onto her back and wrestled the pipe from her hands. 'Some of Boja's flember is in

those crystals!' he yelled. 'Boja, get them *away* from the water!'

Nobbins's clammy hands squished around Dev's waist and hauled him away. 'You don't just come rolling into Darkwater . . .' he wheezed, wrestling him into a head-lock. 'And then take our magical glowing crystals. That's just RUDE.'

'You don't know what they are, what they can *do*!' Dev protested.

'They're going to feed us tonight, that's all I need to know!'

'Thassright.' Elise grinned, creeping closer towards Boja.

He shuffled back, his bottom now teetering over the edge of the jetty.

Slowly, calmly, Elise reached forwards and plucked one of the glowing flemberthysts from his arms. 'Oh, ain't it something,' she marvelled. 'A little piece of magic in such a terrible place like this.'

Then she took another. And another. Once she'd taken them all she spun around in glee.

'LAY THE TABLE, LADS!' she called out. 'DAHLIA IS FEEDIN' US TONIGHT!'

Suddenly a long, dark shape appeared from out of the mist, racing across the rocks and down towards Elise.

In an instant it was upon her, knocking all the bright, glowing flemberthyst crystals out of her arms and into the waters. They hissed and they bubbled, their flember fading beneath the gloom. Elise fell too, catching onto a rock, her legs splashing into the sea just long enough for her thick-soled boots to start dissolving around her feet.

'PRIEST!' Dev shouted.

The long, dark shape lengthened to its full height, its robes flapping around in the wind. 'The sea hungersss,' Priest's voice hissed. 'We must keep it well FED.'

And then, as swiftly as he had arrived, Priest was gone again, scuttling across the rocks and disappearing back into the mist.

Dev slammed his elbow into Nobbins's stomach, pulling himself free and running towards Boja. 'BOJA!' he yelled, trying to drag the bear to his feet. 'How do you feel? Are you OK?'

Boja rolled onto all fours, his extra big floofy limbs barely able to hold him up.

'Ve-e-e-e-ery . . . sle-e-e-e-eepy.'

Dev grabbed Boja's huge sagging eyelids and tried to haul them back open. 'No no no, Boja, you can't sleep here. We have to get you back to the Village. We have to find somewhere safe!'

'You keep that bear *away* from our Village!' Nobbins shouted, pulling Elise to safety.

Dev didn't hear much after that. The wind was becoming even louder. The rain even heavier. The mist even thicker. Within what felt like seconds, the whole coastline had faded from sight, as if it had been scrubbed from the earth itself.

And suddenly Dev could see nothing but Boja, the end of the jetty, and the dark sea swirling around beneath them.

20
A Safe Place

'We can't . . . mmf . . . stay here!' Dev struggled to lift Boja's big, heavy, rain-soaked arm up onto his shoulder as he helped the bear to his feet. Boja yawned a huge, wide yawn, revealing every single one of his glistening teeth. He blinked into the mist. Scratched his head in confusion.

'Duckwater?'

'Darkwater.' Dev nodded. 'It's there, somewhere.'

Dev couldn't see the sea any more, not even the wooden planks beneath his feet. So he led the big sleepy bear away slowly, very very slowly, one foot sliding in front of the other as they made their way back along the creaking jetty and onto the rocks.

From what he could remember, the steps leading up the wall should have been right in front of them. But they too had disappeared.

'I can't tell where we are!' Dev cried, feeling his way along as they stepped from the rocks onto ground that crunched like sand. Burning, black sand, so hot it started to melt the soles of Dev's boots. With a yelp he leapt onto a tumble of large black boulders, and tried to haul Boja alongside. 'We have to go UP!' he shouted over the howling wind. 'We have to get away from the *sea!*'

Boja looked up the rock face, nodded sleepily, and then started to climb. Slowly. Slow-w-w-ly. Dev pressed his whole face into Boja's bottom and pushed from behind. His fur was no longer soft to the touch, no longer puffed out like a well-groomed poodle. The heavy rain had soaked through and now it clung to his skin like a big wet towel.

Finally Boja reached the summit. He collapsed, exhausted. After trying to shoulder-barge a wet bear's bottom up a wall of boulders, Dev was feeling pretty tired too. His skin stung from the sharp rain. His breaths came short and frantic, as he crumpled against the bear's big red belly and looked for any sign of shelter.

And through the mists, he saw a shadow.

It looked so familiar.

It was tall, thick, with *branches* twisting and winding out from its sides.

'The Eden Tree,' Dev gasped, crawling towards it. 'How . . . how did we . . .'

The closer he got, however, the less it looked like the Eden Tree. This wasn't a tree at all, but a huge stone tower, its 'branches' a gaggle of metal pipes poking out from its sides. Realizing what it actually was brought Dev to his feet. 'Keeper!' he puffed, running, throwing himself against its large wooden door. 'Rebecca said Keeper lives in a TOWER!'

He yanked on the door handle but its hefty padlocks rattled back at him. 'KEEPER!' he cried. 'KEEPER, LET US IN!'

No reply came. Dev pulled again on the handle, harder, more desperate.

And then he stopped.

And an idea swirled around inside his head.

'Boja!' He grinned, stepping away. 'Boja! BOJA! Can you help us get inside?'

Boja rose slowly to his feet, mumbled something about waffles, then stumbled sleepily towards the sound of Dev's voice.

'This way,' Dev shouted. 'THIS WAY!'

Boja's weight carried him forwards. Faster. And faster.

At the very last moment Dev jumped aside, as the big, heavy, grumbling bear crashed through the door and then collapsed, into a heap, on the other side.

Dev stepped around him, creeping into the cold shadows of the tower. He helped Boja roll away from the doorframe. Then he lifted the door back up, or at least what bits of it still remained, and tried his best to rest it all back in place.

'Sleepppzzzz,' Boja mumbled, his face pressed into the ground, the rest of his body rumpled into a most uncomfortable-looking position.

A gentle snore whistled through his lips.

'Yes, you sleep.' Dev sat, curling his legs up under his chin, his whole body shaking as all the strains of the last few hours finally kicked in. 'And by the time you wake up,' he whispered, wiping a tear from the corner of his eye, 'I'll have worked out what we do next.'

21
The Beacon

Before Dev could come up with anything even remotely resembling a plan, there came a loud crash from the doorway. A huge, hulking shadow battered its way inside, thick mist swirling in behind.

'WHAT DID YOU DO TO MY DOOR?' it demanded, towering over Dev, lights flickering all across its chest. 'AND WHO SAID YOU COULD COME IN HERE?'

Dev's blood froze. What stood before him looked human, but all its parts were metal. Wires wrapped around wires, valves plugged into valves, thick cables dragged into clattering engines, all of it clamped into place between row upon row of misshapen metal pockets.

Whatever this beast was, its pistons locked and unlocked at regular intervals, its thick bullet fingers flexing as if priming for a fight.

Its head, a grimy, frosted glass bowl, with only a vague swirl of shadows inside, loomed down towards Dev.

'Keeper?' Dev squinted. 'Is that you?'

The glass bowl hissed loudly as it opened, revealing Keeper's grumpy face wedged down inside. Her half-burnt-off eyebrows scrunched down across her broken nose.

'You ARE a robot!' Dev squeaked with delight. 'I KNEW it!'

'NOT A ROBOT!' Keeper grunted, picking an over-stuffed bag up from beside her.

But Dev was too excited to be put off. He got to his feet, marvelling at her robot body, tapping her limbs with his finger and listening out for the TINGs, TUNKs and CLANGs that echoed back.

'Well, you have a VERY robot-y body! How is it powered? Is that why you drink oil? Your lights keep dipping, so they might have loose connections, and I could help you fix that—'

Keeper batted Dev's curious hands away. 'If you must be inside the tower, then you'll both stay down here and be quiet. OK? DOWN. HERE.'

Dev went to reply, but Keeper instantly shushed him. Then she slung her bag over her shoulder, climbed over a stack of unmarked crates and pulled herself up onto the spiral staircase which ran around the wall. CLUNK! CLANK! CLUNK! she stomped, circling the inside of the tower, higher and higher until Dev could barely see her any more, save for a few lights bobbing in the darkness.

Then FZZT! Keeper's lights went out. She muttered and swore.

'You could try . . . rejangling your trobbletrons?' Dev called up. 'I saw you had a few under your armpit. They'll reroute any energy you're not using, and—'

CLANG! Keeper slammed a fist against her chest, and all her lights burst back into life.

'Or, you could just do that.' Dev nodded. 'I wonder where she's going. Boja? Did you see? Keeper's here!'

Boja hadn't seen. Boja was fast

asleep, his lips smacking, his tongue lolling and his paws miming the act of eating a pile of waffles.

'Well, *I* want to see what's up there,' Dev said, patting Boja's fur. 'You stay down here and sleep. I'll go and have a quick look, and then I'll be *right* back.'

He clambered over the crates onto the stairs, leaping two, three steps at a time. Higher he went, higher into the darkness until the steps ran out, and a large metal door stood before him. A cold wind whistled in around it. Dev didn't particularly relish the idea of going back out into the storm, but his curiosity was too much to bear.

He pushed his hand to the door, and he creaked it open.

Instantly the wind spun around him, dragging him out across a metal balcony. He gripped onto the wet railings, his heart in his throat as he leant over and stared down into the swirling mists.

'I heard what you did to their hibbicannon!' Keeper shouted. She stood above him, perched upon a mound of metal planks. 'They've been talking about little else. Well, I'd rather you didn't break anything up here, if that's all right with you.'

Dev noticed Keeper's bag lying beside her feet. A bundle of hibbicus plants spilled out from inside. 'You dig for hibbicus . . .' he said, climbing his way up towards her,

'. . . but I don't think you're making stew with it.'

A smile cracked across the crags and gullies of Keeper's face. She pulled a hibbicus out by its stalk. 'It's to warn the ships,' she replied. 'When they sail too close to Flember Island, they get caught in the mist. They don't see the black rocks of the reef. They don't stand a chance.'

Keeper clicked her metal fingers. A spark flew out from between them, catching upon the hibbicus leaves as they fizzled and crackled like a fuse. She quickly placed the whole plant down into the stone-lined pit in front of her, held Dev back and then – BOOM! – the hibbicus exploded into a bright, dancing fire.

'*I'm* their chance.' Keeper stared into the flames. 'Up here, at the top of this tower, I light the beacon to warn them not to sail too close. All night, every night, and any time the storms come in.'

'That's amazing,' Dev said. 'But what's a *ship*?'

22
The New Beacon

'I'm AWAKE!' Boja boomed from somewhere inside the tower.

Even above the howl of the wind Dev could hear the bear's heavy feet CLOMP-CLOMP-CLOMP-ing their way up the staircase, until finally two eyes bulged out through the doorway. One paw, then two paws clamped onto either side and tried to squeeze the rest of his huge red body through a space clearly not intended for robot bears.

Dev ran down to help. He gripped each of Boja's nostrils, and heaved.

Boja spilled through with a loud POP.

'Boja, are you OK? You were so tired. You . . . you don't

have as much flember as you used to, remember?'

'Am FINE!' Boja smiled a huge goofy grin. He wasn't fine. Now his fur had flattened down again he looked hunched and weak. He smelled weird. One of his eyelids appeared to be opening and closing on its own.

'You . . . you should take it easy. Boja, you mustn't tire yourself out too much.'

'Frrrp!' Boja replied, either from his mouth or his bottom. Dev wasn't quite sure which.

A cry went up from the metal pit. Keeper huddled over the fire, or at least, what was left of it. 'It's hard to keep hibbicus plants alight in this weather,' she complained. 'The wind's too quick up here, too strong, it keeps blowing them out.'

As she spoke, the last flame flickered away.

She reached into her bag and pulled out not one, but two hibbicus plants, placing them both into the pit. 'You asked what a ship was.' She nodded out towards the sea. '*That's* a ship.'

Dev peered out across the sea. The mist lay heavy upon its waters but he could just make out the dark black rocks of the reef, and a faint trail of lights sailing amongst them.

Somewhere in the distance, he heard a 'PARPPPPPP!'

'Ships,' Keeper continued, clicking her fingers. 'Boats.

Vessels full of people, to carry them across the seas. For goodness sake, do you people up on that mountain know *nothing?*'

A spark! It fell upon the hibbicus plants and exploded them both, nearly singeing away what was left of Keeper's eyebrows. She stood back, blowing the smoke from the tip of her nose.

'There are people?' Dev whispered. 'Beyond the island?'

'And that's where they should stay. Far, far away from this place.'

The fire started to flicker. The hibbicus plants were fading already, both of them, as the wind and the rain cut their flames short. 'They're not clear yet,' Keeper muttered, watching the ship's lights drift through the mist. 'We need more *fire*.'

She reached for more hibbicus, but a large pair of red paws pulled the bag away. Boja, swaying a little, his eyes opening and closing at random, grinned like he knew something no one else did. Then he lifted the bag above his head, and tipped all the hibbicus plants down into his open mouth.

'BOJA!' Dev shouted, jumping to grab the bag. 'Boja, what are you DOING?'

Boja rolled one of his eyes down towards Dev, and possibly winked it. 'Helping save *ship*,' he mumbled, a mouthful of black and green pulp sparkling in the back of his throat.

Then his grin disappeared.

His ears pinned back.

And both his eyes sprung wide open.

A rumble sounded from deep inside his belly. Boja clamped his lips shut as if he could stop what was about to come out but it only ballooned into his cheeks, and when they could stretch no more it finally burst through his mouth.

BU-U-U-U-U-U-U-U-R-P-P-P-P!

A huge jet of flame billowed out from between his teeth. It danced high into the air above them, lighting up the mist, blotting the coves and the reef into

bright, blistering view.

'Hurrrrf!' Boja wheezed, wiping a little hibbicus goop from his lips. Then BU-U-U-U-U-U-U-R-P! he went again, igniting the skies as if the sun itself was crashing in through the clouds.

'I've never seen a bear do THAT.' Keeper gazed out to sea, watching the ship as it rapidly changed course to avoid the rocks. Its lights flickered smaller, and smaller, and smaller.

Eventually, even its PARPs faded away into the distance.

She sighed with relief. 'That's one less meal for the sea. Oh, Dev, I could have done with you both being here before now.' She turned and stared admiringly up at Boja. 'I've seen what those waters do to a human. I wouldn't wish it on *anyone*.'

Boja grinned inanely, his top teeth hanging over his bottom lip like a bear with no idea what's going on.

Then, suddenly, a new expression took over his face.

An expression of deep, unrelenting dread.

Dev recognized it instantly.

'We should get inside for this bit,' he said. 'RIGHT NOW.'

He pulled on Keeper's shawls, dragging her down the metal planks and into the safety of the doorway. 'Why

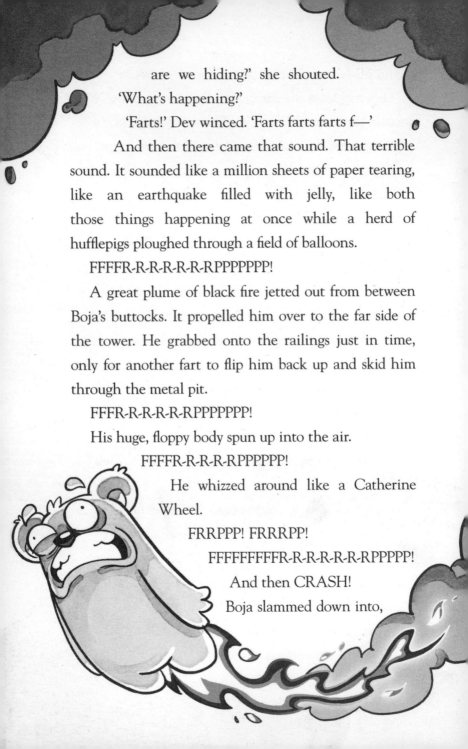

are we hiding?' she shouted.

'What's happening?'

'Farts!' Dev winced. 'Farts farts farts f—'

And then there came that sound. That terrible sound. It sounded like a million sheets of paper tearing, like an earthquake filled with jelly, like both those things happening at once while a herd of hufflepigs ploughed through a field of balloons.

FFFFR-R-R-R-R-RPPPPPPP!

A great plume of black fire jetted out from between Boja's buttocks. It propelled him over to the far side of the tower. He grabbed onto the railings just in time, only for another fart to flip him back up and skid him through the metal pit.

FFFR-R-R-R-R-RPPPPPPP!

His huge, floppy body spun up into the air.

FFFFR-R-R-R-RPPPPPP!

He whizzed around like a Catherine Wheel.

FRRPPP! FRRRPP!

FFFFFFFFFR-R-R-R-R-RPPPPP!

And then CRASH!

Boja slammed down into,

and through, the tower roof. A column of smoke billowed out in his wake. He clonked once, twice, three times against the staircase, the flames sputtering out as his huge, heavy body plummeted to the ground.

Which it then hit, face first, with a sickening THUD.

'Boja!' Dev and Keeper scrambled down the stairs and over the crates as fast as they could. 'Boja, are you OK?'

Boja mumbled something in reply. Something about his nose being squashed.

'Keeper, help me,' Dev said, struggling to roll Boja upright.

But Keeper was distracted. She was staring up to the top of the tower, or at least, where it used to be. Now only burning bits of ceiling remained. It broke away in pieces, little clumps of flaming brick tumbling down towards them.

Clattering against the steps.

Thunking against the ground.

Keeper turned to Dev with a terrified look in her eyes.

And suddenly Dev knew what was inside all the crates.

23
An Awful Fire

The flames danced across the crates, jumping from one to the next, burning through the wood and catching the leaves of all the hibbicus plants stuffed inside.

'You have to get out!' Keeper yelled. She CLANK-CLANK-ed over to Boja and slipped her huge metal arms around his head, while Dev leant into his smoking, charred bottom, and together they heaved the dazed bear through the doorway and out into the mist.

'Further!' Keeper panted.

'Break-faschttt . . .' Boja

mumbled, as his face smeared along the ground.

Once they were at a safe distance, once they'd flumped Boja down onto the rocks, Keeper turned back towards the tower. She watched the thick smoke roll out through its doorway, through the cracks in its shutters, through the gaping great hole in its roof.

And then she started CLANK-CLANK-CLANK-ing back towards it.

'KEEPER!' Dev shouted.

'I have to at least try to put the flames out!' Keeper yelled back. 'I have to save the tower!'

'BUT THE HIBBICUS WILL EXPLODE!'

'I'll be FINE!' she replied, CLUNK-ing her frosted helmet over her head. 'I'm a ROBOT, remember?'

She bowled through the smoke just as – BOOM! – a loud explosion blew the wall out above her. The doorway collapsed beneath tumbling chunks of stone. BOOM! Another explosion. BOOM! BOOM! BOOM! One hibbicus-filled crate after another, tearing apart the walls and bringing the upper levels crumpling down like wet cardboard. What was once a tower swiftly became rubble, a hellish swirl of flame and smoke dancing upon it.

Dev held his breath, staring into the fire for any sign of Keeper.

But he saw nothing.

'Oh, that's nice!' Nobbins stood, admiring the burning tower, his face illuminated in all of its bumpy, lumpy glory. He poked his tongue out to catch a few flakes of burning ash as they flittered down from the sky.

Then he caught sight of Dev and flung his arms out in joy.

'YOU?' Nobbins cheered. 'Did . . . did YOU blow up the tower?'

'Nobbins!' Elise staggered through the mist, her burnt boots FLIP-FLOPP-ing along behind her. 'Nobbins, who is it?'

'The boy.' Nobbins ran towards Dev and gripped him roughly by the cheeks. 'The troublesome boy finally did something *good* for Darkwater!'

Tears glistened in Dev's eyes. '*Keeper* was in the tower!' he cried. 'She . . . she ran back in!'

'Oh, don't worry about that old tin can,' Elise laughed. 'Better for us all if she's gone. All that tower of hers did was warn all the ships away, all them ships with all their gold.'

'Their lovely, shiny gold.' Nobbins waggled Dev's cheeks in glee.

'Well, maybe now they'll start *sinking* again,' Elise snarled. 'Maybe now the sea can chew on their flember and spit their gold out for the rest of us.'

Nobbins dropped Dev to the ground and started to jig, his not inconsiderable frame bouncing around while Elise clapped alongside him. 'What blessed souls are we,' he puffed.

'Catching gold right out of the SEA!' Elise cheered.

Dev stared up at them in utter bemusement.

And his heart sank lower than ever before.

How had he and Boja ever ended up in a place like Darkwater? There was barely a drop of flember here, no sign of the Flember Stream at *all*. Just exploding hibbicus plants, a cruel and hungry sea, and some weird gopple-spider–like man stealing people's flember. And now Keeper was gone. Nobbins and Elise were celebrating. And Boja, Dev's best chance of getting through any of this, was collapsed beside him, thoroughly farted out.

'Darkwater can't be where we're supposed to find the

Flember Stream, it just can't. It must be a mistake. There must be something I'm missing,' he moaned.

Dev huddled against Boja's fur, pulled his backpack off, and lifted the flember book out from inside. Unable to ask Boja to spare any flember, he instead clawed his fingers around the glowing, golden F on the book's cover and wrenched it out from its studs. Flember crackled around his fingertips. It felt warm. He flipped open the book, placed the F down upon the pages of Chapter Two, and watched as the hidden, glowing lines of the map spread out beneath it.

He traced back and forth along the lines, his eyes scanning for anything he might have missed. 'The map must be wrong,' he muttered. 'It *has* to be wrong.'

'Whassat?' Nobbins's huge face appeared over Dev's shoulder. His bulbous nose snuffled like a pig hunting truffles.

'Oh! It's . . . it's just a book.' Dev slammed the covers shut.

'Not that, THAT.' Nobbins grabbed the golden F and held it up to the light of the burning tower. With a dirty finger he smeared thick black circles around his eyes, as if he was drawing on a pair of spectacles. 'It . . . it looks like GOLD.'

'Give it back.' Dev leapt up, only for Nobbins to kick him to the ground.

'You had GOLD all along!' He bit his rotten teeth into it. 'And it's solid too.'

Elise grabbed the F. 'Every day we're served that stew,' she hissed. 'That filthy *mucky* stew. It gets into your blood, you know. It eats away at you from the inside.'

Nobbins snatched the golden F back and started staggering away from the coastline. 'But gold . . .' He beamed. 'Gold buys us *real* food. Food the sea ain't touched.'

'Dahlia will be MOST pleased with us.' Elise limped after him. 'Most pleased INDEED!'

Dev sprang back onto his feet and started shaking the sleepy bear behind him. 'Boja, get up,' he insisted. 'Boja, *please*.'

A large red eyelid heaved open. 'Hungry,' Boja whined.

'Me too. And we'll find food soon. Proper food.' Dev slid the book inside his backpack and pulled it onto his shoulders. 'Not just food, but the Flember Stream. You need its flember now as much as the Eden Tree does. We'll find it all.'

He glowered after Nobbins and Elise.

'And those two are going to lead us right to it.'

24
The Sanctuary

The rain across Darkwater eased, as if it were stepping aside to let the tower burn in peace.

The winds calmed.

The mists faded.

With the vague promise of food now rumbling in his belly, Boja rolled himself onto his bottom, up onto his feet, and then trudged sleepily along behind Dev. Together they followed Nobbins and Elise around the outer ring and then down to the next. And again to the next. Down through the rings of the quarry, tiptoeing carefully between the hibbicus leaves, Boja moaning, grumbling and huffing all the way.

Once at the deepest point of the quarry, where the

thick column of rock rose up from its centre, Nobbins and Elise started the climb up towards the Sanctuary.

They bickered and they chuckled, snatching the golden F from each other as they clambered from one platform to the next. Soon they were stepping out into the daylight, running towards the entrance to the mines.

'Quickly,' Elise hissed, bustling Nobbins against its doors. 'Before the boy follows us in.'

'Don't worry, dear.' Nobbins held his nametag up to the mysterious box on the wall. Its light flashed from red to green, and with a great rumble the doors started to slide apart. 'I wouldn't let a troublemaker like that any-where *near* the Sanctuary.'

Dev was already near. 'The *nametags*.' he gasped, crouching behind a pylon. 'So *that's* how they get inside the mines.'

Once Nobbins and then Elise had slipped out of sight, and the doors had started closing again, Dev took his chance. He raced towards the building, skidding down onto his knees and sliding in through the thinnest of gaps.

The doors loudly CLUNK-ed shut behind him.

His scarf was trapped.

As he was pulling it out, he heard sounds coming from the other side of the doors. Huffs. Puffs. Grumblings about breakfast. Dev pressed his face against the slit between the doors to see Boja staggering up the last of the platforms.

'Boja!' he squeaked. 'Boja, stay where you are. I'll find you a nametag, I'll get you inside!'

'Boo . . .' Boja puffed. 'BOOOO . . .'

'What is it? What are you trying to say?'

'BOOM!' The exhausted bear flumped his bottom down into the wet mud. 'Boom! Boom boom boom!'

Now Dev could hear it too.

BOOM!

BOOM!

BOOM!

He followed the wall around, finding a thin crack through which he could look out towards the coastline. The tower was still burning. Dark flaming ash fell from the sky like snow. It was landing on the leaves of the hibbicus plants, lighting them, exploding them, and blowing wide holes in the rock. Dev watched as explosion after explosion flung out hot, flaming chunks of hibbicus, which then lit the other hibbicus nearby. Suddenly the jagged outer wall of the quarry crumbled away.

And black sea water roared in through the hole.

25
Food

Dev rushed back to the doors. 'Change of plan. Get back to the Village!' he shouted, trying to force them open. 'Boja, can you hear me?'

One of Boja's eyes looked up, but the other looked all over the place.

'The sea's coming in! You have to get to safety! Get back to the Village and I'll find you there!'

Boja nodded, grunted, farted, stood up, then staggered back towards the platforms. For such a huge bear he now looked weak, and so utterly confused by everything.

'And then we'll find you some more flember,' Dev sighed. 'Somehow we will, I promise.'

He turned back inside the Sanctuary. 'Nobbins!' he

hissed through the darkness. 'Elise! We have to get back
to the Village too!'

It was cold in there, a shadowy graveyard of once
powerful mining machinery, rusting drills, spikes and
clamps all poking out from the darkness. Dev tiptoed
between them, heading towards a beam of murky daylight
that shone in through the broken rafters of the ceiling.

It fell upon a shallow pit in the ground.

In the middle of which stood a small wooden hut.

It seemed such an odd place for a hut to be. Its walls
were wooden, its blue roof tiles missing in places, and the
weathervane on top was bent and pointing all manner
of wrong ways. It had been draped with lengths of split
rope. Black, polished rocks inscribed with Dahlia's name
had been rolled around its base, with pile upon pile of
scrap-metal flowers scattered between them.

'Nobbins! Elise!' Dev called down to the two figures huddled beside the hut. 'WE HAVE TO GO!'

Nobbins nearly jumped out of his skin, before stepping in front of Elise and waggling a chubby finger up towards Dev. 'YOUUUU . . . you're not ALLOWED in here!'

Behind him, Elise hurriedly creaked the hut's little wooden door open. She bent down, placed the golden F carefully inside, then closed the door again. 'He won't stop us now,' she smirked, slamming her hand against a large red button on the wall. 'The Foodbringer has been *summoned*.'

The hut rumbled and shook, a great cacophony of noise rising up from beneath it as if the gears of the earth itself were grinding together.

And then . . . PING!

Elise gripped onto the door and swung it open. A high-pitched squeak of joy whistled from between her lips.

For there, inside the hut, was a mine cart.

With a single glass jar inside it.

'BATTERED BEEF BUTTOCKS!'

Elise cried. She grabbed the jar, twisted its lid off, sank two fingers into its thick yellow oil and pulled out a glistening brown slice of meat.

Nobbins forgot all about Dev, and spun around to see what she'd found. 'Oh, blessed Dahlia!' he whimpered, scrubbing off his glasses and redrawing his eyebrows higher than ever before.

'*Blessed* Dahlia,' Elise agreed, cramming the slice between her teeth and chewing as if she'd never eaten food before. Nobbins grabbed the jar, wedging his own pudgy fingers inside and slobbering an oily slice down his gullet. 'MMMMM!' he squealed, slumping down and rolling back and forth on his ample bottom. 'I haven't taschted beef buttocksch in scho, scho *long*!'

'This isn't the time to be *eating*!' Dev shouted. 'We have to GO!'

They both stopped mid-chew, and stared up at the boy on the edge of the pit.

'You DARE,' Nobbins spluttered. 'You dare schtep inschide the Schanctuary, and then INTERRUPT usch while we're enjoying Dahlia'sch schweet FRUITSCH—'

He didn't get to finish his sentence. A stray hibbicus plant sailed in through the open ceiling, its leaves fizzing like a fuse. It DONK-DONK-DONK-ed across the roof of Dahlia's hut and then PLOMP-ed right down in front of Nobbins.

He stared at it, slowly redrawing a curious expression above his eyes.

And then BOOM!

The hibbicus exploded in a bright flash of light. It blew Dahlia's hut into pieces, before bringing a midsection of the ceiling crashing down upon the pit.

Dev was thrown backwards, rolling across the ground like a floppy sock. His head pounded. His limbs trembled. But still he slowly crawled toward the pit, looking to see if Nobbins and Elise were OK. Finally he spotted them pinned beneath a twisted metal rafter. The jar was in front of them, smashed, while one last battered beef buttock lay just out of reach.

'MINE!' Nobbins shouted. 'It's MINE MINE MINE!'

'No, it's MINE!' Elise shouted back, her arm straining to claw at the buttock. 'You could do with eatin' less! This one's MINE!'

Nobbins called up to Dev. 'Here, lad, you're a good boy. Kick us that bit of food, would you? To me. It's mine.'

'Leave it behind,' Dev said, sliding down into the pit. 'We have to get out of here!' It took all the strength he had left, but he managed, at least, to shift the rafter enough that they could both wiggle free. With not even a grunt of thanks, Nobbins scrambled like a cluttercrab towards the beef buttock. Elise was instantly upon him, sticking her fingers up his nostrils.

'MINE!' they both shrieked. 'MIIIIINE!'

More explosions sounded outside.

The Sanctuary creaked loudly above them.

Nobbins and Elise stared at each other in panic.

'*You* have it!' Nobbins suddenly squealed, scrambling away from the battered buttock, slipping and tumbling over the rubble.

'No, *you*!' Elise replied, chasing after him. 'You stay here and eat it. Enjoy yourself!' They pushed and shoved

each other through the shadows of the Sanctuary.
Nobbins got to the doors first, swiped his nametag for
them to open, then squeezed out between them. Elise
was right behind, calling Nobbins every rude name she
could think of.

Dev followed as fast as his shaking legs could manage.
The doors had already started closing again, but then a
rafter clattered down from above, wedging itself between
them and leaving enough space for Dev to throw himself
through.

The explosions were getting closer. The coastline was being demolished. Sea water circled the outer ring, running a full lap around the quarry before spilling over the rocks and splashing down into the ring below.

Where it dissolved everything it touched.

Dev hoped upon hope that Boja had already made it back to the Village. That he might see the big red bear standing up on the cliff top, waving back at him. Or just face-down and asleep, that would be fine too.

'Please please please.' Dev gazed towards the cliff. 'Oh, please, Boja, say you got back safely.'

'HI, DEV!' Boja yelled from behind him. Dev swung around, back towards the Sanctuary. There, through the crumpled metal doors, through the rubble and the dust, sitting upon a mound of collapsed roof, was Boja.

Gleefully chomping into the last battered buttock.

Dev opened his mouth to shout, just as more sparkling hibbicus plants sailed down from the sky, landing PLOMP-PLOMP-PLOMP around the grinning bear.

And then . . .

26
Something Like a Plan

The explosion raced through the doors in a cloud of dust. It flung Dev backwards, knocking the breath out of his lungs and slamming his body over the metal railings. He reached out just in time to grab the platform below, but in doing so pulled its bolts out from the rock – PING PING PING! – and it started sliding down the other platforms like a sledge.

Suddenly a great screeching noise echoed around the quarry. Dev looked up to see the scaffolding above him start to buckle. The higher platforms tore free, crashing down behind him in a flurry of metal and dust.

'Oh, FLIP!' he yelped, gripping tighter onto his platform and willing it to slide faster. 'Oh, FLIP FLIP FLIP!'

With a loud CLANG and a spray of bright sparks, Dev's platform finally bounced across solid ground. He breathed a huge sigh of relief, only to inhale sharply again as he skidded over a cluster of hibbicus leaves. They sparkled and fizzed, and before he could scramble free they exploded, throwing him from his platform and rolling him across the mud.

Right into the burnt-out shell of the hibbicannon.

He paused for a moment to catch his breath, as bits of rock TINK-TINK-TINK-ed down above him. And then, through the clouds of dust, he saw movement. Two figures, clambering up the higher rings of the quarry. Bickering and shoving each other as they went.

'Nobbins! Elise!' Dev crawled out from his shell. 'Help me! I need to get back up to Boja!'

'You're on yer own!' Nobbins yelled, just as the bridge he was climbing over started crumpling into the sea water.

Elise did nothing to help, instead using Nobbins as a stepping stone to reach higher ground. 'This is *your* mess, lad!' she shouted. 'You can help yourself out of it!'

A loud explosion sounded behind Dev. He turned to see a tall metal tower, high upon the second ring, its foundations buckling as it splashed down into the water. Waves spilled down into the ring below. Only a few more and the sea would be flooding into the very bottom of the quarry.

It would reach *Dev.*

He hauled himself onto his feet, searching through the broken machinery around him. 'I can get back up there,' he muttered to himself. 'I can *use* this stuff to get back up to Boja.'

Invention ideas popped into his head. A rocket pack. Clambering metallic legs. A slingshot, to fire himself back into whatever was left of the Sanctuary. His mind started to run away with him. He imagined crawling through the rubble, a tuft of red fur poking out in front of him.

He'd pull on it.

And it would be Boja.

And he'd still be asking about breakfast.

Dev looked down at the few pieces he'd picked up. A rusted old pipe, and the bottom half of a flopperwodget.

His heart sank.

'Oh, who am I kidding?' he cried, flinging them both to the ground. 'This is all just useless junk! I can't use it for anything!' He kicked the side of the hibbicannon. 'Even the things I *do* make don't work. I flung *this* thing up into the sky. I drowned all the tools I brought with me. And *you* . . .' He slammed his fist against the front hoop of his backpack straps to try and make the Portable Airbag inflate. It clanked, and it ground, but nothing came out. 'You only seem to work when you WANT TO!'

He collapsed to the ground, shaking. 'I *need* to get to Boja,' he sobbed, clawing at the wet mud. 'I just don't know HOW.'

'Are you going to spend all night crying?' a muffled voice called out. 'Because if you are I might throw myself back into the sea.'

Keeper, or at least, the top half of Keeper, tumbled over the lowest ring and crashed onto the ground.

Dev stared at her in disbelief. 'You . . . you SURVIVED!'

Keeper didn't look quite so cheerful. 'Sea got my legs,' she grumbled, clanging a fist against her hips. A nest of singed pipes poked out where her legs used to be. 'Let's hope it chokes on them.'

Dev had never been so happy to see anyone in his life. He ran towards her, pulling her safely away from the spray of the sea. Her helmet was shattered, her red cheeks now blackened from the mud, and she looked utterly exhausted.

'So, where's your friend?'

Tears welled in Dev's eyes again. 'He was in the Sanctuary, but it collapsed. Then everything around it collapsed. But I have to get to him, Keeper! I have to find Boja!'

'The upper rings are flooded, Dev. Unless you have some brilliant idea to get us up there, to get us to any higher ground, we're completely *trapped*.'

'I'm working on it.' Dev picked the flopperwodget back up and waggled it. 'I'll come up with something.'

A sly smile cracked into Keeper's cheek. 'I think you already did.' She pushed herself upright and leant onto her arms, walking on them as if they were legs. Then she stopped beside the remains of the hibbicannon.

'The . . . the hibbicannon?' Dev asked. 'But that's for making stew.'

'How did it get all the way out here then?'

'I . . . I blew it up!'

Keeper's smile widened.

'I blew it *up!*' Dev gasped. 'Maybe I can do that again, but this time with us *on it!*'

'It'll be risky,' Keeper said.

'It'll be FINE!' Dev cheered, clearly forgetting all the times it had never been fine.

27
First Launch

'The good news' – Keeper lay beneath the huge hole in the hibbicannon's main chamber – 'is that most of its working parts are still, well, working.'

'We need to *aim* the explosion,' Dev nodded, pacing round in a circle. 'Not just up, but *forwards* too.'

'BOOSTERS!' they both shouted at the same time.

'We have the parts.' Dev rushed around, picking up all the rusted bits of metal he could find. 'We can make the most of what's around us. Build the hibbicannon into some sort of . . .'

'Hibbi . . . rocket?'

'The Hibbirocket!' Dev cried. 'But *this* time we have to get it absolutely right. When I was rebuilding the hibbicannon I tried to make it work like Boja's belly; hibbicus goes in, flames comes out, but I missed something. I *forgot* something.'

He stopped. His mouth fell open. And Dev P. Everdew realized the one thing the hibbicannon had been missing.

'It needs a BOTTOM.'

'A . . . oh, a what?' Keeper looked a little disgusted.

'Boja didn't just belch flames, he farted them too. It's the last explosion that comes out of him. But I didn't build anything to release that explosion from the hibbicannon, that's why it blew up!' He clenched his fists with determination. 'This time, I'll make it FART.'

There was a loud crash from further up the quarry. The sea had eaten its way through one of the carriages between the third and fourth rings, and was spilling down between them like a waterfall.

Dev's pulse quickened. 'Although this would be *a lot* easier if I had some tools.'

'What do you need?' Keeper turned the brace around her neck, and every metal pocket on her body sprung open. All thirty-seven of them. She started pulling out tools. 'Got a . . . clickwidget. A larpspoon. Nicklefidgets, ocklestops, oh, even a spindlefrump.'

Dev stared at each tool like they were flavours of ice cream. He grabbed the ones he recognized, and a few of

the ones he didn't, dumped an armful of junk beside the hibbicannon and they both set to work. Keeper patched up the holes. Dev built a bottom.

INVENTION 504: The Hibbirocket

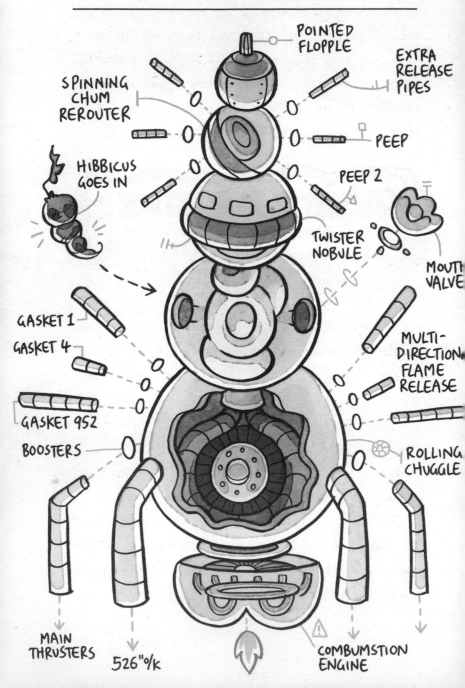

POINTED FLOPPLE

EXTRA RELEASE PIPES

SPINNING CHUM REROUTER

PEEP

HIBBICUS GOES IN

PEEP 2

TWISTER NOBULE

MOUTH VALVE

GASKET 1

GASKET 4

MULTI-DIRECTION FLAME RELEASE

GASKET 952

BOOSTERS

ROLLING CHUGGLE

MAIN THRUSTERS

526"°/k

COMBUMSTION ENGINE

At first they worked in silence, but after a while Dev's curiosity got the better of him. 'Are you a robot?' he asked.

Keeper twisted a few more nicklefidgets inside the hibbicannon's tighter compartments, before a smidgen of pride crept into her face. She reached into one of her open pockets and pulled out a crumpled square of cloth.

CHARLOTTE KOPERSTICK
-OUTER RINGS MECHANIC (B-CLASS)
WILBURFORCE MINING CORPORATION

'I'm as human as you are, Dev.'

'But you drink oil!' Dev protested. 'And you clank-clank-clank around in a big metal body!'

Keeper glanced nervously up to the fourth ring, watching the spray of the sea as it splashed over the edges. 'I'll tell you how it happened, Dev, but only if you *hurry with that bottom.*'

Dev nodded, eagerly hammering rivets into each crumpled buttock.

'Well, I followed Albert Wilburforce to Darkwater for the same reason any of us did,' Keeper started. 'We all wanted to work the mines. We were told we'd be hugely rewarded for it, and, at first, it was a happy enough life.

Darkwater looked very different then, Dev. We had trees, actual *trees*, orchards filled with plums, oranges, even fuzzapples. Small plots of land for vegetables, goats, enough to keep us all fed. The machines dug away in the quarry. The miners worked away on the machines. With Wilburforce in charge we all lived happily. We became a *community*.'

Her voice fell. A bitterness crept in.

'That is until the food disappeared.'

'Because you dug up the flemberthysts?' Dev said.

'I suppose that was the start of it, when the trees stopped bearing fruit. Then the trees themselves started to die. The ground gave us nothing but rotten vegetables. That would have been bad enough, but then what food we had in store started to go missing too.'

Dev gasped. 'Someone stole it?'

A nicklefidget pinged out, hitting Keeper in the forehead. She clutched it, swearing, as a line of crimson trickled out between her metal fingers.

'Helmut,' she muttered. 'Or *Priest*, as he calls himself. He looked different in those days. Bigger. *Wider*. Seemed to only be growing while we were all going hungry. Wilburforce realized it was Priest stealing all our food for himself so, while Priest was away, Wilburforce went into that cave of his and took the food back. Crates of the stuff. Then he hid it all where Priest wouldn't find it.'

Dev noticed a small, oily black tear wobbling in the corner of Keeper's eye.

'Wilburforce cornered Priest out on one of the jetties. He was furious. They both were. They argued, both of them getting angrier and angrier. One of them grabbed the other and then . . . well, then Wilburforce fell. He tumbled into the sea with an almighty splash. I was working the outer rings nearby, I was close enough to jump in after him – which I did, Dev. I did it without even thinking. Couple of seconds later I remembered why we don't go in the water. It burns, Dev. It really, *really* burns.'

More explosions made Dev jump. A line of rusted pylons crashed down above them. Black sea water raced around the fourth ring and then sploshed and bubbled its way over the edge, down to the fifth.

Dev and Keeper both worked even faster. Keeper kept on talking, as if she was relieved someone was finally listening.

'I couldn't find Wilburforce, not a trace, the sea was too quick to claim him,' Keeper continued. 'I barely managed to pull myself out. I called to Priest for help but he was just standing there, terrified, shouting that the sea had taken flember – it had taken Wilburforce, and that now it would come for the rest of us. Well I had to get away. I dragged what was left of my body all the way back up to the Village – it gave Rebecca the shock of her life, I can tell you – and once I started to recover I did the only thing I could do. I rebuilt myself. All the bits of me the sea had taken, I replaced with scrap, junk, whatever I could find. Made myself a body that didn't even need food any more, just runs on oil and fumes.'

She slammed her compartment shut. 'You work with what you've got,' she puffed. 'Isn't that right?'

Dev gazed at her, his mouth agape, his mind barely able to process the story he'd just heard. 'You . . . built yourself?' He gasped.

Keeper reached past him, grabbing the large metal bottom from between his trembling fingers. 'Is this done? DEV. IS THIS DONE?'

Dev nodded silently, unable to stop staring at her.

'Well then,' Keeper huffed, tightening the bottom onto the base of the Hibbirocket. 'I think we're DONE!'

With a loud SPLASH, sea water spilled over the lowest ring. Ominous black puddles widened across the ground, creeping towards them both. 'FUEL!' Dev cried, clonking his fist against his helmet. 'The Hibbirocket still needs fuel!'

Keeper grinned, reaching into a pocket on her shoulder and pulling out a smear of black and green mulch. 'I told you, hibbicus is good for blowing things up,' she said. 'So I always keep a little of Rebecca's disgusting stew on me, just in case I need it.'

She slapped a glob down into the Hibbirocket's mouth valve. Then, with Dev's help, she wrapped a length of chain around herself, binding her upper half to its side.

'It's going to be a bumpy ride,' Dev shouted, wrapping the end of the chain around his forearm and pulling it taut.

'It's the landing I'm more worried about.' Keeper winked, clicking her metal fingers until a spark flew out. It sailed towards the valve and then down inside the Hibbirocket, bouncing across the stew. It sparkled and fizzed and then – BOOM! – the Hibbirocket's main boosters fired, wrenching it up, dragging Dev off the ground before he'd had the chance to take a breath.

28
The Flight of the Hibbirocket

Once it had cleared the Sanctuary, the Hibbirocket's flames sputtered out. For a few terrifying moments Dev, Keeper and their hastily cobbled-together invention all hung in mid-air, as though they might tumble right back down into the quarry. Then, FFFFR-R-R-R-RPPPP! The Hibbirocket's huge metal bottom shuddered into life, farting out a great blast of black fire and propelling them across the sky.

Away from the Sanctuary.

Over the Village.

Towards the dark, bustling trees of the Wildening.

Dev's end of the chain started to unravel, his body swinging helplessly against the sides of the Hibbirocket.

Then the black flame sputtered out too. Keeper shouted something, but it was garbled noise, muffled by the crash and crunch of treetops. By the time it came to a stop the Hibbirocket had been flipped around and was tangled in a mesh of branches, hanging high off the ground like a huge, gestating gumpworm.

Dev dangled some distance below it, the tips of his boots skimming against soft, wet grass.

'We went too far!' he gasped, finally getting his breath back.

'I NOTICED!' Keeper yelled. She struggled to get free from her chains, but they were wrapped too tight. 'You're going to have to climb up, Dev, work this thing out of the trees.'

The black scratches across Dev's arm started to throb. Memories of the Wildening came flooding back. The chase. The panic. The shrieking, the snarling, the thunderous crashing. The terrifying creatures slinking through the darkness.

And then he realized he could hear it all now *too*.

The sound of trees swaying, *ripping*, somewhere in the depths of the Wildening, as if something very large was making its way towards them.

'Dev!' Keeper cried. 'Dev, get this thing DOWN!'

'I can't!' Dev replied. 'It's too high. It's too heavy!'

The noises came again. Louder now. Closer.

'Well, we can't stay HERE!'

'No, we can't.' Dev replied, just as a familiarly over-ambitious thought started to alight inside his brain. 'But I might know a way out. Keeper! Do you have any more of Rebecca's stew?'

Keeper popped open her shoulder pocket and scraped out the last few globs.

'We're pointing in roughly the right direction,' Dev replied. 'We could always . . .'

'. . . *ride* it out. Oh, Dev, I DO like how your mind works!' Keeper stretched as far as she could, dripping the stew into the Hibbirocket's mouth valve. Then she clicked her metal fingers above it. Once. Twice. A third

time.

'Quicklyyyy!' Dev called up, as the trees around them started swaying, groaning, creaking, a great rush of wind blasting through the branches. 'QUICKLYYYY!'

SKKKK! Sparks lit from Keeper's fingers down to the stew, instantly igniting it. BOOM! Fire blasted through the Hibbirocket's boosters, wrenching it out from the trees and skidding it along the ground. Dev had precious few seconds to clamber on board before the rocket's oversized bottom rattled and shook and then FFRR-R-R-R-R-R-R-RPPPPP! Another mighty black fire blasted out, speeding them through the Wildening.

Dev dragged himself up towards the thinner nozzles of the Hibbirocket, clinging onto its outlet pipes as if he was riding a hufflepig. Tears streamed from his eyes as they rocketed faster, and faster, until suddenly he could see the edge of the quarry wall.

And then PUTT!

The flames sputtered out into thick bulges of grey smoke.

Dev gritted his teeth, clenching his fists tight around the pipes.

'WE'RE GOING OVER!' he yelled as the Wildening disappeared behind them.

Then CLANG! The Hibbirocket hit the Village roof, a bright shower of sparks trailing out behind it. It skipped like a stone before spinning back into the air, sailing between two pylons and scraping down along their chains.

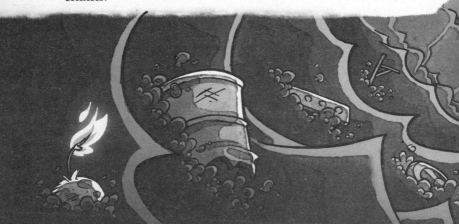

Then the chains ran out.

Dev could see nothing below them but the quarry. Or at least, where the quarry had once been. Now it looked more like a lake, filled almost to the top with the crashing, bubbling waters of the pitch-black sea. Dev clung to the Hibbirocket even tighter. The idea of plunging into the waves filled him with dread, but he quickly realized they weren't falling at all, they were still very much speeding through the air, the Hibbirocket's bottom having farted out such a blast that its momentum was carrying them all the way towards the Sanctuary. It caught against the outstretched pylons, circling its collapsed roof before spinning down inside. Then it CLANG-ed and DONK-ed off the buckled supports before finally embedding itself, nozzle-first, in a huge mound of rubble.

Everything fell deathly still.

After a little while, Dev unscrunched his eyes. After a little while longer, he unclenched his fingers. His body slid down to the ground, his heart pounding, his lungs gasping, his legs shaking.

No, it wasn't just his legs.

The rubble was shaking too.

A deafening rumble filled the air, and suddenly the Hibbirocket was sinking at speed, swallowed into the ground and dragging everything, and everyone, with it. Dev scrambled for safety, but anything he could hold onto was sliding down with him. He grabbed at the front hoop of his backpack straps, praying *this time* the Portable Airbag might kick in just when he needed it.

But no, still nothing.

Instead, his flimsy body disappeared inside a cloud of dust.

Down through the floor of the Sanctuary.

Down, into Darkwater's mines.

29
The Mines

When Dev opened his eyes again everything had quietened. Grit pattered down around him. Dust billowed gently by. A huge open cavern stretched high above, its rocky walls pockmarked with dark hollows from which railway tracks, or at least the remains of them, wilted down like tree roots. And between them all hung the Hibbirocket, its battered body wrapped up in cables and suspended four or five storeys from the ground.

'HOOOOOOOO!' Keeper, still strapped to its side, gasped herself awake. As she did the Hibbirocket suddenly shunted down another level, bringing with it a flurry of rocks and mud.

Dev slid down a sloping pile of rubble and ran

beneath the Hibbirocket. 'Keeper!' His voice echoed around them both. 'Keeper, are you OK?'

'Your *bear*, Dev!' Keeper coughed. 'You might want to hurry up and find him before this whole place comes down.'

Another rumble through the cavern.

Dev nodded and backed away from the Hibbirocket, cautiously feeling his way across the uneven ground. He peered into the shadowy holes, the crevices, the hollows.

'Boja? Are you down here?'

Suddenly he spotted an eye staring back at him.

A glassy, watering eye.

'You hear it too now, don't you?' Priest's spindly limbs unfolded out from the darkness. 'The ssssea. It cries out in hunger. It pleads. It ROARS.'

Another rumble. A CRA-A-A-ACK in the rocky wall. A spray of black water gushed through, pooling behind Priest and burning the hem of his robes.

'PRIEST! YOU KEEP AWAY FROM DEV!' Keeper shouted, swinging helplessly above them. 'I'll not lose anyone else to the sea like I did with Wilburforce!'

Priest recoiled at the name. 'W . . . Wilburforce,' he replied, his bottom lip trembling. 'Wilburforce *fell*. His foot slipped, then the sea just took him, took him for his flember. I couldn't do anything, I couldn't *reach* him!' He turned to Dev, his cruel face now suddenly etched with worry. 'I've tried to keep us safe ever since, lad, really I have. I used the crystals, same as I did with you, I used them on everyone, like I said. Took some of their flember away – small amounts, TINY amounts. They didn't miss it. They got a bit tired, that's all.'

He backed Dev against the wall. 'Then I fed that flember to the sea. It's flember the sea wants. I told you, it's hungry for *flember*. I thought that if I kept feeding it morsels then it wouldn't have to take anyone else like it took Wilburforce!'

'DEV, RUN!' Keeper shouted. 'Get AWAY from him!'

Another rumble.

The crack widened.

The spray of water became like a jet,

Dev tried to move but Priest was instantly upon him, grabbing his scarf and hauling him back against the wall. 'Please,' Dev cried. 'I didn't want any of this! I only came to Darkwater looking for the Flember Stream. I only came down here looking for Boja!'

'The sea's already had a taste of your monster's

flember.' Priest grimaced. 'I thought that would be enough, but it's just hungry for more.'

Another rumble. The jet widened. Bubbling black sea water trickled around the edges of the cavern, hissing against Dev's boots. The sound sent a cold panic prickling across his skin. He slammed his hand against the front hoop of his backpack straps, again and again, hoping, *pleading* with the Portable Airbag to start working again.

'There's no use fighting it, lad.' Priest whispered. ' I failed. I didn't feed the sea enough of our flember, and now it's coming for us all.'

'Not me,' Dev growled, punching his fist so hard against his chest it smashed the hoop. With a great FW-P-P-P-P-P the Portable Airbag inflated around him, flinging Priest back across the cavern and spinning the flember book out into the air.

And then down again, right into Dev's open hands.

Priest staggered below the tip of the Hibbirocket, his robes trailing along the water's edge. He paused, just for a moment, lifting his head and staring at Dev with a curious admiration.

His thin black lips stretched into a grin.

'Your flember's *strong*, lad,' Priest said, wrenching the flemberthyst crystals from around his neck. 'I took a little of it, but you still have *so much* left.'

He held the crystals into the jet of water and watched as they hissed and cracked, the faint glow of his own flember fading from inside them. Soon they had dissolved away into nothing. He sighed, slumping down to the ground. His breathing slowed. His head bowed.

'Maybe you'll find a better way to save this town than me.'

Then there came the loudest rumble of all.

The crack in the wall widened.

And what looked like an entire ocean roared in on top of Helmut J. Priest.

30
Tunnels

Dev, still clutching the flember book, quickly clambered up the rocky walls. It wasn't easy with one airbag wobbling out in front of him, another dragging behind, and the sea crashing around his heels, but he managed to roll inside a wide gap in the rocks before kneeling, exhausted, upon some buckled railway tracks.

'You're in one of the access tunnels!' Keeper shouted over the roar of the waves. 'They run through the whole mine. If your bear's still in here, that'll be how you find him!'

Dev stuffed the airbags back down inside his backpack, squeezed the book between them, and crawled to the edge. The cavern below was flooding, the tip of the Hibbirocket suspended just a metre or so above the swirling waters.

'Keeper! I can't just leave you here!'

'Oh, don't worry about me! If the sea tries to chew this rusted body up again, then I'll just rebuild it.' Keeper winked. 'As long as it leaves me an arm to work with.'

A loud cracking sound rippled around the cavern. The walls heaved under the weight of the water behind them. Dev tried to think of an idea, any idea, something ingenious to save Keeper.

But he couldn't focus.

Everything was so *noisy*.

'Dev, you have to GO!'

'I'll find Boja,' Dev replied. 'Then we'll come back for you. *He'll* be able to get you free from the Hibbirocket!'

'Sure, SURE!' Keeper shouted over the roar of the waters. 'Just GO!'

'We'll come back for you!' Dev yelled, spinning upon

his heels and feeling his way into the tunnel.

Dev stumbled on through the dark, trailing his fingertips along the cold, wet rock, tripping over discarded pickaxes and lanterns and bumping into upturned mine carts. Soon he couldn't even hear the sea any more, only the sound of his own breathing and the pounding of his nervous heart.

Suddenly he saw a wisp of light.

Just a sliver.

It moved across the wall like a glint of moonlight.

Dev reached out his hand, and it crawled across his fingers.

'Silverfish,' he gasped. He knew silverfish from Eden. He'd find them slithering around in the darker, damper corners of his cupboards. They were tiny little creatures with with tiny little bodies and tiny little legs, and they glowed with their own shimmering light. As he placed it back onto the wall, other silverfish flowed along with it, until soon a whole cluster of thin glowing lights guided the way.

Then, suddenly, Dev came to a halt. A pile of boulders was stacked from ground to ceiling and completely blocking his path.

There came another rumble.

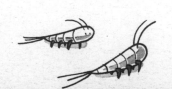

The sound of waves echoed behind him.

'The sea's inside the tunnels,' he cried, watching as the silverfish frantically scattered between the boulders. He tried to follow, hauling the smaller rocks away before clambering onto the larger ones, desperate to squeeze between them, when suddenly, they all dislodged at once.

With a scream Dev rolled forwards, tumbling into a cave just seconds before a torrent of loud, hissing sea water gushed in behind him. He scrambled up and out of the way just in time, clambering onto a ledge and huddling into a ball.

By the low light of the silverfish he could just make out his surroundings. The path had given way to a collection of sharp, rocky clusters, each falling away into gaping great chasms. One such chasm claimed the sea. What were once rolling, crashing waves had now become a black waterfall tumbling down into the gloom.

Dev huddled tighter.

And he started shivering.

He wished, more than ever before, that he was back in Eden. Back in the warm, familiar surroundings of his workshop, tinkering with some ridiculous new invention that would inevitably collapse, blow up, or try to fly towards the sun. Then, when the evening drew in, his mum would knock on his door and leave a plate of fried duck eggs and wildertoast for him to eat.

His stomach groaned hungrily at the thought of it.

'I never should have left,' Dev whimpered. 'I never should have even set foot in the Wildening. I got so excited about chasing the Flember Stream, about saving the Eden Tree, I didn't think how hard it might be.'

He wiped at a tear with the heel of his hand. 'I'm sorry, Boja,' he sniffed. 'I'm sorry I ever dragged you into this.'

The light from the silverfish started to wane. They were moving. With tears still glistening in his eyes Dev watched them swarm across the ceiling, bustling between the stalactites. And slowly, carefully, he started crawling along below them. The rocks were slippery, the chasms either side were *endlessly* deep, but right now he'd risk all of that rather than stay here, alone, in the darkness.

And it wasn't long before he saw what they were heading towards.

There was a faint glow up ahead. It spilled out from a crack in the rocks, a crack just wide enough for Dev to squeeze through.

The glow brightened around him.

'Flemberthyst crystals!' he gasped.

They studded the walls, the ground, the ceiling. A

mist of beautiful blue flember wisped between them, an ebb and flow of light, drifting, dancing and sparkling through the air. Dev lifted his hand and felt it shimmer around his fingers. It felt warm. It felt *healing.* And the further he crawled, the brighter the flember shone, until he reached a hole filled with a light so brilliant that it almost hurt his eyes to look.

But that didn't stop him.

He poked his head right through it.

Dev squinted. He could see something red. Something lumpy.

Excitement swelled inside his chest.

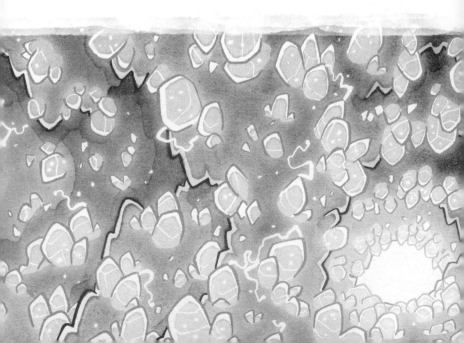

'BOJA!' he yelled.

The red lump waved back.

'HI, DEV!'

Dev rubbed his eyes, blinking furiously against the light to try and work out where they both were.

And slowly, very slowly, things faded into view.

Laid out before him was an enormous underground chamber. Huge chunks of flemberthyst hung from the ceiling like chandeliers, flember swirling, swaying, swishing between them, humming through the crystals as if they were singing. Rich, green, dew-soaked grass covered the ground, with hedges, bushes, ferns and flowers, the most *beautiful* flowers, scattered out across them. And rising out from the middle of it all Dev saw a cluster of flemberthysts arranged in a ring, holding a pool of clear, shimmering water.

In which sat Boja.

With a very healthy grin on his face.

31
Dahlia

Two loudspeakers crackled into life.

'ALL HAIL,' came a voice. 'DAHLIA, THE FOODBRINGER, IS UPON YOU.'

Dev instinctively ducked down as music started playing through the chamber. Weird, plinky-plunky music. A metal gate in the far wall rattled open, and a dinky little train puff-puff-puffed its way along a set of tracks. It circled the floor of the cavern, a chain of mine carts dragging along behind it.

'All hail, Dahli-a-a-a-a!' the train driver sang along with the music. 'She is so great, so wise, and so beautiful, and so bri-i-i-lliant . . .'

The train screeched to a halt. The driver stumbled

out from the cab, and stepped into the light of the flemberthysts.

She arranged her gown.

She stood tall.

At least, as tall as a little girl could stand.

She looked younger than Dev, with large blue eyes, wide rosy cheeks, and bundle upon bundle of light blonde hair curled around her face. Her elaborate gown, stitched from a number of different colourful fabrics and then lavishly decorated with feathers, was clearly way too big for her, but she wore it with an intense pride.

And then there was the gold.

From where he was crouched Dev could see a crown upon her head – no, wait, *three* crowns, stacked upon each other. Gold necklaces draped from her neck, gold bracelets around her wrists, gold rings upon her fingers and all manner of gold brooches pinned to her gown.

Her pockets jangled with every step she took.

'BIG SILLY BEAR! I, GRACIOUS, BEAUTIFUL DAHLIA, SHALL BRING YOU HIGH TEA.' Dahlia pulled out a golden tray and walked to the crates against the wall. The *crates*. In all the splendour of the flemberthysts, all the joy of seeing Boja again, Dev had barely even noticed the crates. Loads of them, maybe a hundred, each packed full of glass jars.

'MMMMM.' Dahlia thought for a moment, then headed towards the crate marked *Pastries*. 'Let's see, you look like a bear who would appreciate' – she pulled out a jar, unscrewed its lid and tipped a plump, current-studded bun onto her tray – 'a FUDDLEBUN.'

Boja's tongue lolloped down, and a long string of drool dipped into the water.

Dahlia pulled out more jars, piling their contents high upon her tray. Ramblepounds, lippincakes and fluffy pink bufflechips. Marshmallow-topped cornets. Chocolate-covered thicks, flups, flips, raspberry chomps and peach delights. And then there were the biscuits. Oh, the biscuits. Lemon puffs, garibaldis and pifflesweats, knock-cheese flats and a seemingly endless stream of pistachio-rippled snuckleflomps.

While Dahlia was distracted Dev took his chance to climb down. He leant through the gap, as discreetly as he could, only for the rock he was leaning on to suddenly dislodge beneath his hands. Without warning his entire body slipped forwards, and with an almighty yell he tumbled all the way down the wall, finally coming to rest in a crate marked *Mixed Pickles*.

He pulled himself out. Brushed himself down. And put a few jars of jellied sausage and minced fidgets back into their crate as he stood back up.

Dahlia, her tray heaving with pastries, stared at Dev like one might stare at a gallumping snotworm.

'WHAT ARE YOU?' she cried.

'My name's—'

'I DON'T CARE!' she screamed again. 'You are NOT allowed down here. This is the house of the FOODBRINGER!' She reached up to her tray and threw a ramblepound, which clonked off Dev's helmet. 'THAT'S ME! I AM THE BLESSED FOODBRINGER!'

Whizz! A pifflesweat.

'BEAUTIFUL . . .'

A bittlecrunch.

'AMAZING . . .'

An oat plopping.

'DAHLIA!'

Dev batted his way past, defending himself as best he could against the onslaught of pastries. Once he had climbed up and into the flemberthyst pool, he splashed through the water, wading towards Boja and slamming his face into the bear's soggy fur.

'I thought I'd lost you,' he whispered, a lump in his throat. 'Boja, I was so scared.'

Boja gulped down a stray lemon puff and wrapped his big furry arms around Dev. Tighter he squeezed, and tighter. Bright, beautiful blue flember circled around them both, prickling Boja's fur on end, crackling across Dev's skin and sinking down, right down into his bones.

The most blissful feeling rushed through his whole body.

And all his aches gently ebbed away.

'And you look *so* much better than when I last saw you,' Dev smiled. 'You're full of flember again! You've refilled!'

Bubbles popped up around Boja's bottom.

'Yeah, you're definitely back to normal!' Dev laughed.

'Not me!' Boja protested. More bubbles rippled up. Dev peered into the clear water and there, underneath Boja's buttocks, he saw a crack in the flemberthysts.

A crack from which the brightest light of all was shining.

'You've found it,' he gasped. 'Boja, you've found the Flember Stream!'

Before either of them could get too excited, however, a great cracking sound echoed through the chamber. Dev looked up just in time to see the Hibbirocket spear down through the flemberthyst ceiling. 'Boja—' he started, but Boja's arm was already around his waist, hauling him out of the pool just as a calamitous avalanche of dust, rocks and crystals splashed into its waters. The pointy end of the Hibbirocket followed, stopping just centimetres above the pool, its entire weight suspended by a mass of tangled cables.

Keeper, what was left of her body now even more battered than before, finally wrestled free from her chains and tumbled down into what remained of the pool.

'Ohhhh, that's better,' she sighed, sweeping her hair from her eyes. Then a thin trickle of sea water spilled down through the Hibbirocket.

And the beautiful clear water around her started to turn black.

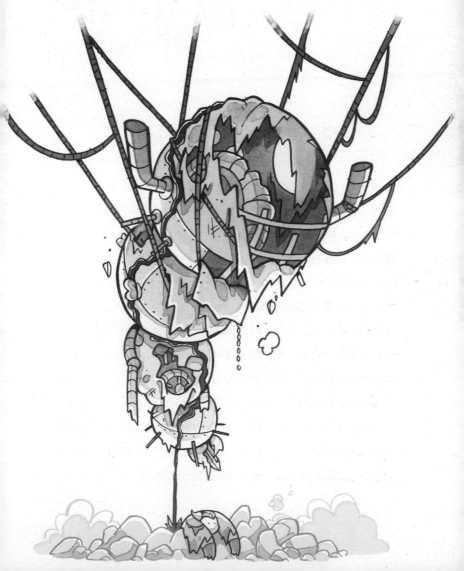

32
Darkwater's Last Hope

Keeper splashed and flailed and crawled out of the pool just as the Hibbirocket finally broke free of its cables, crashing down behind her. It brought with it half of the ceiling, an almighty roar of crystal and rock that buried the pool, buried the crack in the flemberthysts, and buried the Flember Stream underneath.

'We were so close!' Dev cried from the safety of Boja's arms. 'We *found* the Flember Stream. We could have gone *home!*'

He watched as poisonous black sea water gushed in through the ceiling, dissolving the flemberthysts as if they were sugar lumps.

'We could have gone home,' he sighed.

'WHO'S THIS NOW?' Dahlia screamed, waggling an angry finger towards a wheezing, exhausted Keeper. 'SHE'S not allowed down here EITHER!'

Dev slipped out from Boja's hold and the two of them ran to help Keeper, dragging her upper half away from the waters while Dahlia angrily hopped along beside. They rolled her crumpled metal body up onto higher rocks and there she lay, staring at the flickering lights above them.

'So you found what was left of Darkwater's flember, did you?' She coughed. 'Buried all the way down here? And here we all are, just in time to watch it all be swallowed up by the sea.'

Dahlia started flicking her in the head, as if she wasn't sure Keeper was real 'YOU,' she demanded. 'You're in the presence of DAHLIA THE FOODBRINGER, and you are NOT WELCOME.'

Keeper gazed up, blinked, and blinked again. 'I must have fallen harder than I thought, Dev. I swear I can see a little girl saying her name is Dahlia.'

Dev was busy in his own thoughts. 'There must be a way to save the flember,' he muttered. 'We can't let the sea take it *all*.'

He stopped, and triumphantly clonked his fist against his helmet.

'So we'll just have to take the flember FIRST!'

He swung around towards Boja. Boja, however, had been preoccupied. He had found a jar of lippincakes and pulled one out, but after sticking his paw in for another it had become stuck.

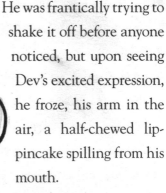

He was frantically trying to shake it off before anyone noticed, but upon seeing Dev's excited expression, he froze, his arm in the air, a half-chewed lippincake spilling from his mouth.

'Gmphuh?' he replied.

'Boja, you have just enough flember to keep you alive, but on the day I made you I accidentally filled you with the flember from a whole *mountaintop*! Do you remember? When you were all bright and sparkly? And then you tried to put it all back into the Eden Tree?'

Boja's mouth rose and fell through a succession of smiles and frowns as he remembered what had happened. 'FWOOOOSH!' he finally cheered, raising both arms triumphantly above his head.

'Fwoosh exactly!' Dev grinned. 'And then we came all this way to borrow a bit more . . .'

'Flember!' Boja cheered.

'From the . . .'

'Flember Stream!'

Dev clapped with joy. 'YEAH! And you were going to carry that flember back to Eden, remember? Well, we can't reach the Flember Stream now, but there's still flember you can carry. Up there, in the flemberthysts. Can you take it, Boja? Take the flember and hold onto it, keep it safe until we can find our way back to the surface?'

'He . . . he can do that?' Keeper asked.

'Boja's pretty amazing.' Dev beamed with pride.

The cavern shook again. The glistening black water-fall bulged, splashing out across the grass. The bushes, the flowers, all of them crinkled away before Dev's eyes. 'Boja!' An urgency filled Dev's voice. 'Boja, we don't have long!'

'CAN DO IT!' Boja yelled, excited to be helping out. He clenched his paw so tightly the glass jar shattered around it. He slammed another fistful of lippincakes into his mouth, and thrust both his sticky paws up again towards the ceiling. 'HNNNNNGHHHH!' he growled, furiously waggling his fingers.

A beautiful blue glow smoked out from the flember-thysts. It sparkled and it shimmered, then swirled into a cloud, a sparkling river of lights trailing down towards Boja. It wrapped itself around his paws, up his arms, until soon his whole body was cracking and flowing with Darkwater's flember.

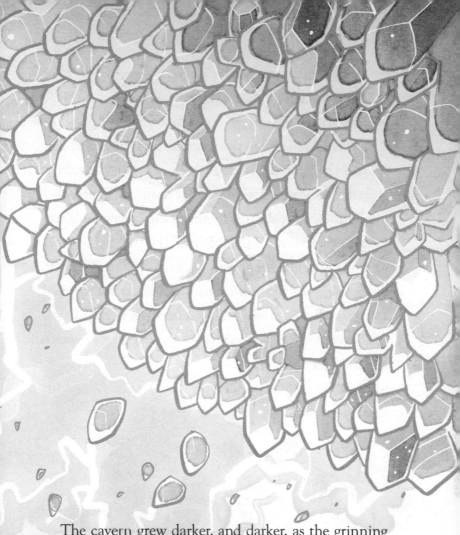

The cavern grew darker, and darker, as the grinning
bear grew brighter, and brighter.

Dahlia broke the silence. 'YOU! YOU ... SAVAGES!'
she screamed. 'You come here UNINVITED, you tear
down the ceiling, you RUIN my high tea! And now you
STEAL ALL MY PRETTY LIGHTS!'

She stormed away, carefully avoiding the sea water as she climbed back inside the cabin of her little train. 'Well, you can all just STAY here and clean up your MESS,' she said sulkily, yanking on the levers in front of her.

The train PHEEP-ed loudly.

Puffs of steam chuff-chuffed out from its chimney.

'Dahlia must know a way out of here,' Dev said. 'Boja! Grab Keeper!'

Boja, still glowing with bright, crackling flember, hauled Keeper's top half over his shoulder and followed Dev towards the train. Dahlia yelped in panic. 'Come ON!' she snarled, the train sl-o-w-l-y shuffling forwards. 'COME ONNNNN!'

Dev caught up, bundling into the cart behind her. Boja ran alongside, dropping Keeper into the next cart, before tumbling into the last. He had, somehow, also found the time to scoop up a few more jars of food, which he hugged proudly.

'GET OUT!' Dahlia shouted, as the train trundled a lap around the sea water. 'THIS IS NOT FOR YOU! YOU CAN'T COME!'

'Dahlia, if you know how to get back above ground then we need to come too!' Dev shouted. 'The mines are *FLOODING!*'

As if to prove his point a loud CR-A-A-ACK echoed throughout the cavern. Dev looked up in horror to see the ceiling bulge, then give way completely, all the faded flemberthyst crystals crashing to the ground as a torrent of dark black water burnt through them. It roared like a wild beast, swirling, raging, racing towards the train.

Dahlia's sweet little train.

'PHEEEP!' it whistled again, merrily puff-puffing back through its gate, and deeper into the mines.

33
The Bridge

The train clattered along, lurching and swaying and even, at one point, spinning round in a loop-the-loop. And then the tracks started to climb. A slow, rattly, nerve-racking climb, the train wobbling and clattering as it puff-puffed its way through narrow tunnels of rock. Dev clung onto the sides of his cart, his teeth clenched, his heart pounding.

The sound of the sea echoing in his ears.

It crashed and swirled behind them, lashing against the tunnel walls and throwing a sharp spray out from the darkness.

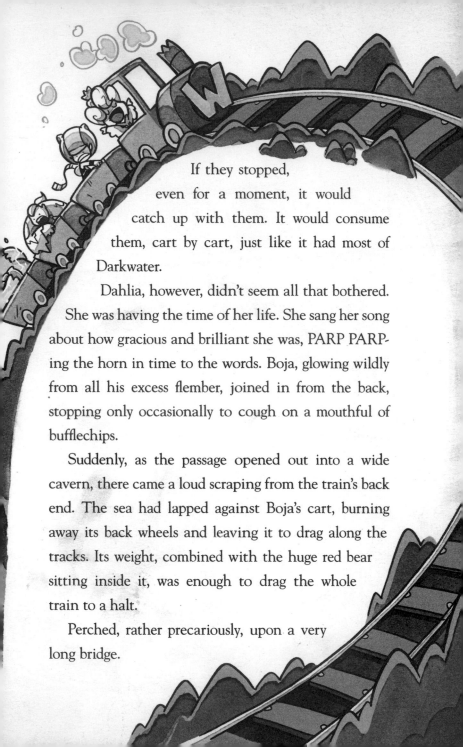

If they stopped,
even for a moment, it would
catch up with them. It would consume
them, cart by cart, just like it had most of
Darkwater.

Dahlia, however, didn't seem all that bothered.
She was having the time of her life. She sang her song
about how gracious and brilliant she was, PARP PARP-
ing the horn in time to the words. Boja, glowing wildly
from all his excess flember, joined in from the back,
stopping only occasionally to cough on a mouthful of
bufflechips.

Suddenly, as the passage opened out into a wide
cavern, there came a loud scraping from the train's back
end. The sea had lapped against Boja's cart, burning
away its back wheels and leaving it to drag along the
tracks. Its weight, combined with the huge red bear
sitting inside it, was enough to drag the whole
train to a halt.

Perched, rather precariously, upon a very
long bridge.

'YOU'RE ALL SLOWING ME DOWN!' Dahlia screamed, shuffling her bum back and forth as she urged the train on. It puffed and it whined. It whined and it puffed. Suddenly the hook connecting Boja's cart to the next pinged itself loose, giving the train an unexpected burst of speed. The engine lurched forwards. Its wheels locked. It twisted across the tracks. And then, in an instant, it was tipping over the edge.

'DAHLIA!' Dev grabbed the neck of Dahlia's gown, pulling her into his cart just as the engine disappeared off the bridge. It dragged his cart along with it. Without taking a breath he flung Dahlia towards Keeper and he leapt from his cart into theirs just as it started to shunt along too. Keeper was quick to roll herself and Dahlia out the back, but Dev was too far behind. As the second cart was dragged over, all he could do was throw himself out and into the air.

'HOOOOF!' he yelled, his fingers grabbing onto the tracks. A fire blazed through his muscles as he hauled himself up, his body rolling alongside the one remaining cart. Boja was sat inside it, his ears pinned back, his cheeks filled with marshmallow-topped cornets.

'Devvv?' Boja coughed.

'I'm OK, Boja.' Dev laughed with relief. 'Just give me a minute to catch my breath.'

'I don't think we have a minute.' Keeper pointed back to the tunnel they had come in by, to the sea water gushing through. It spilled down into the cavern below them, bubbling and hissing across the uneven ground. It chewed at the wooden legs of the bridge until – CRA-A-A-ACK! – the first leg gave way, pulling the tracks behind them down into a slump.

'NO!' Dahlia screamed, wrenching free from Keeper's arms. 'I'm not STAYING here with any of YOU! I'm getting out of here by MYSELF.' She turned away from the cart and started stomping further along the bridge. Arms out, fingers waggling, heading towards an archway at the far end.

'Dahlia, be careful!' Dev rose to his knees. 'It'd be safer if we leave together.'

'HA! As IF! You losers can stay ri-i-i-ight HERE!' Dahlia yelled back. 'Everything was just FINE until you showed up!'

She raised her nose haughtily in the air just as the bridge's second leg gave way behind them all. Sleepers clattered away behind Boja's cart. They splashed loudly into the water, then disappeared down into the darkness.

Dahlia shrieked, then waddled even faster along the tracks.

'This bridge won't stay standing for long.' Dev grabbed onto Boja's paw. 'Boja, grab Keeper, we'll follow Dahlia!'

'Wait wait wait, maybe there's a quicker way out.' Keeper turned the brace around her neck, and all her pockets flipped open. She pulled out the contents. Nicklefidgets, screwdrivers, bolts, wires, cogs. Small buzzing, whirring contraptions. Ocklestops. A clicky-widget. Magnifying lenses, bulbs, oil canisters, a couple of metal fingers (spares, Dev assumed). Folded scraps of paper. A locket. A bundle of hair.

She grumbled and swore, flinging each item down into the water.

And then, from the largest pocket on her back, she pulled out a tiny, withered, rather mouldy-looking hibbicus plant.

'I always kept a spare for the tower.' She grinned. 'May as well use it for *something*.'

Dev instantly knew what she was thinking.

'We can't,' he gasped.

'We *have* to,' she replied, holding the hibbicus up in front of Boja's nose.

34
An Escape

'Boja, I need you to listen,' Dev started. 'I know when you ate hibbicus before it made you feel really bad, but—'

Boja didn't wait to be talked into it. He CHOMP-ed his teeth down around Keeper's fingers, gulping both the hibbicus – and three of her metal fingers – down without hesitation.

He patted his belly. A puff of grey smoke wisped out from his nostrils.

'QUICKLY!' Dev shouted, just as more of the bridge's legs started to crack and creak below them. 'We'll have to grab Dahlia on the way!' He heaved Keeper up inside Boja's cart, then tumbled in alongside her, listening

INVENTION 505: The Belch-Powered Minecart

HIBBICUS

INSERT INTO MOUTH CANAL

520°°

PHASE 1:

INITIAL EXPULSION (BELCH)

PROPELS CART @ 9,627°/kb

FLAPIPLEX TONGUE!

CHEWING DENTURES

INTEGRATE MULCH

① ② ③

PHASE 2:

FULL EXPULSION (BOTTOM) SINGLE EXPLOSIVE BURST

PROPELS CART - MIN. OF 56,724°/kb

119⁼

POSSIBLE AFTER EFFECTS:
- SINGED FUR
- NOXIOUS SMELLS
- SORE BUTTOCKS

EXPLOSIVE CORE (BELLY)

← ----------------------------------- ⊢

POTENTIAL DISTANCE COVERED: 157mp

nervously as the hibbicus bubbled and gurgled inside Boja's stomach.

'Turn round, Boja. Face the other WAY!'

Boja did as he was told, turning around in the mine-cart and gripping onto the back of it. And yet, even as its fiery heat rose up into Boja's throat, even as his eyes bulged with panic, the big red bear couldn't help but giggle.

'Hee-hee-hee-OOO-U-U-U-U-R-R-R-R-P-P-P-P!'

A great blast of fire billowed out from his mouth. Their cart may have only had a front set of wheels but still it rocketed along the tracks at an almighty speed, bright sparks spraying out from behind it, and at least two of its occupants screaming with terror.

'DAHLIA!' Dev yelled as they clattered towards the little girl. 'DAHLIA, GET READY!'

'B-U-U-U-U-U-U-R-P-P-P-P-P-P!' Boja belched again, propelling them even faster. Dahlia turned round just as Dev grabbed her, lifting her from the tracks and handing her back to Keeper.

'PUT ME DOWN!' Dahlia screamed, kicking Keeper in the nose. Then she stared up at Boja, and she giggled. 'Why . . . why's the bear pulling that face?'

Dev turned his head to see what she was laughing at. Boja, facing forward now, looked pained. Unsure. One of his eyelids was fluttering. He chewed on his lower lip, gripped tightly onto either side of the cart, and stuck his bottom out behind him.

'Here it comes,' Dev winced.

FFFFRR-R-R-R-R-R-R-R-R-R-R-RPPPPPPP!

It was a bigger fart than Dev had ever heard

before, echoing around the cavern as if it was cheering them on. A column of black flame tumbled out from between Boja's buttocks, powering their cart across the tracks and flinging it through the archway just as the entire bridge collapsed away behind them.

35
Whatever is Left

The skies above Darkwater were calm. There were no storms rolling in. No mist. No rain. Just the early light of dawn, quietly breaking the clouds into a beautiful array of pinks and yellows.

What had once been a quarry was now just a cove. All the towers, the pylons, even the Sanctuary itself had been lost to the pitch-black seas. In fact, the only part of Darkwater left standing was the Village, the large, metallic bun perched upon its mound of rusted scrap. It tilted, a Hibbirocket having bounced off its roof during the night, and now its highest gangway served as a viewing platform for all the miners to stand on.

They stood, in silence, and stared across where

Darkwater used to be.

Suddenly the gangway started to wobble. Panicked, the miners scrambled back inside, only for the metal bun itself to crack free of its supports and slide down the mound. The mound, too, trembled, then collapsed, its pieces scattering across the ground as two large metal doors opened up from beneath it.

And a mine cart skidded out.

Even though he was actually delighted to see daylight again, Dev's face had been frozen into a look of sheer terror. His eyes were wide, his cheeks stretched back, and Boja, meanwhile, was frowning. His nose was scrunched up. His bottom lip poked out. He looked like he was concentrating really, really hard.

And then . . .

FRRP!

One last, tiny bumsqueak rolled the cart a few centimetres further.

'ALL DONE!' Boja grinned, reaching forwards to

squeeze Dev up into a hug. Instantly the warm, crackling glow of Boja's flember brought life back into Dev's limbs. He took a deep breath and curled into Boja's fur.

'That BEAR!' Cled shouted, clambering out from the crumpled Village. 'He did it AGAIN! Knocked our Village right over this time!'

Rebecca wasn't far behind. She pushed past Cled, tears streaming down her cheeks. 'Dev! I thought you were lost! I thought you were under the waves!'

Before she could reach him, however, Dahlia bundled out in front of her. She stood, bustled her gown, and glared at Rebecca with the most furious of expressions. 'TAKE ME TO MY DADDY!' she demanded.

'Your . . . daddy?' Rebecca stuttered, struggling to process her thoughts.

'My DADDY,' Dahlia insisted. 'He's taller than me, and he's older than me, and he's *fatter* than me, and he has BIG FLUFFY CHEEKS!' She mimed hairy sideburns with her fingers.

Rebecca stared at her in disbelief. 'That sounds like . . .'

'. . . Albert Wilburforce!' Dev gasped.

'My DADDY!' Dahlia shouted. 'He brought me all my *food*. Then he went back up to the surface. He said he wouldn't be long, but he's been *a-a-a-ages*.' A thunder

billowed across her face. 'And he is going to be SO
ANGRY when he finds out what you did!'

'Never mind who her daddy is.' Prickles stumbled
between them. 'Look at her! She's covered in GOLD!'

Grippins pushed him out of the way, grabbing one of
Dahlia's three crowns and holding it up to the sunlight.
Then he too was shoved aside, as both Nobbins and Elise
crowded around the little girl. 'Ohhh, we'll be rewarded
WELL for this!' Nobbins slobbered, drawing a pair of
devious eyebrows upon his forehead. 'We'll take all this
gold straight to Dahlia.'

Elise gazed over to where the Sanctuary used to be.
'Where IS Dahlia?'

Dahlia snorted indignantly, and wasted no time in
punching Elise hard on the leg, and Nobbins even harder

in the stomach. While they both wheezed and crumpled to the floor, she snatched her crown back from Grippins and perched it back upon her head. 'I'm Dahlia, stupid! And this is MY gold.' She backed against the cart, fists clenched. 'I traded food for it. It's MINE, FAIR AND SQUARE.'

Something she was wearing caught Dev's eye too. The golden F from the front of the flember book. It was clamped to her gown like a brooch, still crackling and glowing with flember.

'But *that*' – Dev swiped the F – 'is *mine*.' Dahlia swung around, preparing to punch someone, but as she did Boja tightened his arms protectively around Dev. His eyes blazed. His nose crumpled. All the extra flember he was carrying crackled around him like an electrical storm.

The assembled crowd of miners shuffled back in awe.

'He looks so . . . magical,' Rebecca gasped. She reached out towards the glowing red bear, and watched in amazement as flember sparkled around her hand. 'Dev, what *happened* down there?'

With a great moan, Keeper heaved herself out from underneath Boja's buttocks. She tumbled over the side of the cart, crumpling to the ground in a loud hiss of steam. 'They found the last of Darkwater's flember,' she puffed, lifting her head and squinting out towards the sea. 'Just

a shame there's no Darkwater left to make any use of it.'

Dev slipped out from Boja's arms and helped Keeper sit upright against the cart.

'Well, you got what you wanted.' She smiled. 'A whole load of flember to take back to your village. You can go home, Dev, go home and save your tree.'

The thought of going home made Dev's stomach leap with joy. He'd see his mother again, Santoro, Ventillo, Mina and all his friends. He'd sleep in his own bed. He'd eat duck eggs and wildertoast, *so much* duck eggs and wildertoast, with hot sweet tea on the side. But most importantly of all, he'd lead Boja up to Shady Acres, and with Darkwater's flember they'd finally bring the Eden Tree back to life.

And then everything would be *fixed*.

He looked up to Boja, bright, glowing Boja, who

grinned back in sheer delight. 'Go . . . home?' Boja asked.

'I think we can.'

Boja yelped excitedly, his whole body sparkling with flember. Dev stood with a cheer in his heart, as he turned to say goodbye to Rebecca, to Cled, to all the miners huddled in front of their collapsed Village.

And then he saw their dirty faces.

Their blackened lips.

Their torn, weathered overalls. Their home now just a small, dusty cliff top covered in rusting metal. And somewhere, deep inside, he realized what they had to do.

'But this is *Darkwater's* flember,' he muttered.

'Eden Tree!' Boja proudly gurgled. 'Take it . . . for the Eden Tree!'

'Boja, we can't.' Dev clutched his paw. 'It belongs here. They've been so long without it, we can't just carry it away now!'

Boja's excited face slumped into a frown. 'But . . . we go . . . *home.*'

'We will. We WILL. But first we have to give Darkwater their flember back.' A smile crept between Dev's cheeks. 'And I think I know how we can do it.'

36
The Garden

Dev paced around, his mind lost in thought, his fingers fiddling with the glowing, golden F in his hands.

'Ohhhhh no,' Cled shouted. 'I recognize that face. He's coming up with another invention. He'll blow something up, or he'll make that bear fart, or . . . or . . .'

Cled was absolutely right, Dev *was* thinking about an invention. But this time there would be no explosions, no metal bottoms, no flying off into the Wildening. This time he already had everything he needed right here.

'We need to recreate the Flember Stream, but *above ground*,' he muttered. 'And to do that, we'll need . . .'

He stopped, swung around, and pointed a finger at

Dahlia.

Panicking, she clung onto her jewellery.

'BOJA!' Dev beamed, now thoroughly enjoying the thrill of a new invention whizzing around inside his head. 'All the flember you took from the caves, from the crystals, I need you to give it all to DAHLIA!'

The miners looked confused. Dahlia looked confused. And Boja looked most confused of all.

Dev's voice fell to a whisper. 'Please, Boja, trust me.'

Boja huffed. Then he nodded and held out his arms, his fur rippling as a mist of beautiful blue flember flowed across them. To the amazement of all those watching, it swirled into the air, shimmering like the starlight, before wafting down upon Dahlia. Or, more specifically, upon all her golden jewellery: her crowns, her necklaces, everything weighing down inside her pockets.

All of it now crackling with the magical light of flember.

'I . . . look . . . MAGNIFICENT!' she boomed.

'Gold acts like a battery.' Dev started pacing again. 'It'll *hold* all of Darkwater's flember. It'll be your own version of the Flember Stream. But to use it, we'll also need something to draw that flember *out* of the gold, to move it around, to conduct it. And to do *that*, we'll need flemberthysts . . .'

279

He paused. Something glimmered inside his mind. It was a memory of something Priest had told him.

He said he'd been taking flember from *everyone*.

'Could you all please turn out your pockets?' Dev asked.

The miners looked at each other, confused.

'Snap to it,' Rebecca ordered with a clap, pulling mostly cutlery from hers. Forks, spoons, and then a small, glowing flemberthyst. 'How . . . how did *that* get in there?'

'I've got one in my hat!' Prickles yelped, slipping a crystal out from behind its buckles.

'I found one too!' Grippins tipped a crystal out from his boot.

'We had them all along?' Elise gazed at her own lumpy, glowing crystal.

'Priest hid them on you,' Dev said. 'He hid them on all of you! They've been slowly taking small amounts of your flember.' He held Rebecca's flemberthyst away from her, watching as its swirling, glowing flember slowly drifted out, rose like a cloud and then sunk back into her heart.

Rebecca's cheeks flushed with colour. Her chest heaved with a relaxed sigh.

'Well that feels a *lot* better.' She smiled.

'Me next!' Nobbins demanded, as Dev took his flemberthyst. Then flemberthysts from Cled, Grippins,

Prickles and all the other miners, pausing just long enough for the crystals to return their flember where it belonged.

As each miner breathed a long, contented sigh.

'Right.' Dev beamed. 'Now . . .'

'BEHHHH!'

He swung round to see a small goat. Its fur was matted, its legs wobbling, and a gently glowing flemberthyst was clamped between its two yellow teeth.

'Mean Fervus!' Dev grinned. 'You made it out!'

'FEVVUS!' Boja shrieked, running towards the little goat and grabbing it up into a hug so huge, so furry, that soon no one could see any goat in there at all. Dev reached in, plucking Mean Fervus's flemberthyst from between Boja's arms and waiting for its faint wisps of flember to waft back towards the goat.

'Thank you, Fervus.' He smiled. 'As I was saying, now these flemberthysts aren't taking your flember, they can channel *Darkwater's* flember instead. From the gold, through the flemberthysts, and all the way into . . .' He thrust a hand into his own pocket, and pulled out his last pepper, his last mini cauliflower, his last spricket, and his last flonion. '. . . FOOD!' He grinned.

INVENTION 506: The Flember-Filled Garden

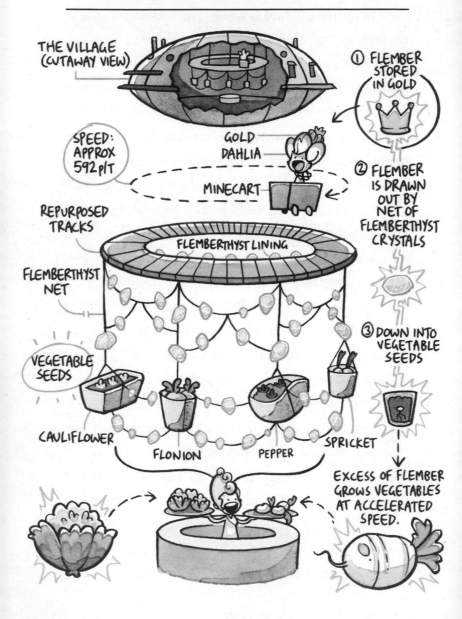

THE VILLAGE (CUTAWAY VIEW)

① FLEMBER STORED IN GOLD

SPEED: APPROX 592 p/T

GOLD DAHLIA

② FLEMBER IS DRAWN OUT BY NET OF FLEMBERTHYST CRYSTALS

MINECART

REPURPOSED TRACKS

FLEMBERTHYST LINING

FLEMBERTHYST NET

VEGETABLE SEEDS

③ DOWN INTO VEGETABLE SEEDS

CAULIFLOWER

FLONION

PEPPER

SPRICKET

EXCESS OF FLEMBER GROWS VEGETABLES AT ACCELERATED SPEED.

'FLONION SOUP!' Rebecca yelled across the bar some hours later. 'Third helpings, if anyone wants any.'

Every miner inside the Garden cheered, grabbing at the bowls of hot, steaming soup as they were passed from table to table. Dev took one, Boja took three. Even Mean Fervus got a whole bowl to himself, which he sat in. Still there was plenty to go around. Thanks to the magic of flember, and the rather ingenious apparatus Dev had built to channel it, the few withered vegetables he'd pulled from his pocket had not only grown plump and healthy, but also offered up a bounty of seeds.

Seeds which, with the help of some extra flember, grew quickly into even more plump healthy vegetables.

'IS ANYONE LISTENING TO ME?' Dahlia yelled from high above them all. She waggled a frying pan around like a weapon. 'THIS MAN'S BORING. SEND SOMEONE ELSE UP!'

Nobbins clambered down the ladder to ground level. 'Someone else's turn to go and keep her amused,' he grumbled, rubbing the bruises on his head.

Elise duly took her turn, getting a poke in the eye the moment Dahlia's cart whizzed past her.

'Cauliflower and spricket stew next, I think,' Rebecca grinned, clutching a crate full of fresh sprickets. She admired the bubbling pots on the stove, taking a deep breath of all the delicious smells around her. 'Oh, Dev, thanks to you we have food like we could only have dreamt of!'

Dev scraped the last spoonful of soup into his mouth, then licked the bowl clean. 'We're making the most of it too.' He beamed. 'Filling up before we leave.'

'Leave?' Rebecca gasped.

'Leave?' Boja echoed, a lump of flonion tumbling from his mouth.

'LEAVE?' the other miners shouted.

'We . . . we have to,' Dev stammered. 'We still need to find the Flember Stream, and we can't reach it from Darkwater anymore!'

'But . . . but . . .' Rebecca panicked. 'Where would you go? Dev, where else is there to look for it?'

Dev pulled the flember book from his backpack. He opened it onto the bar, and flipped to Chapter Three. Then he pulled the glowing, golden F from his pocket and ran it across the pages. The lines of the map emerged, twisting and turning, winding through the whole chapter until the very end, where they all stopped inside a circle.

A circle marked with one word.

'*Prosperity*,' Dev whispered.

Rebecca's pale eyes stared into his as if she was

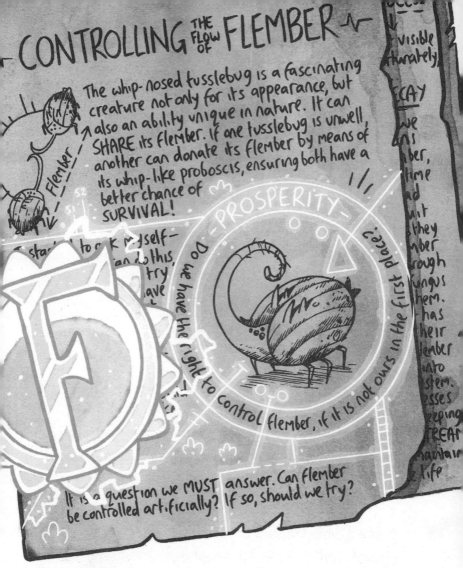

CONTROLLING THE FLOW OF FLEMBER

The whip-nosed tusslebug is a fascinating creature not only for its appearance, but also an ability unique in nature. It can SHARE its flember. If one tusslebug is unwell, another can donate its flember by means of its whip-like proboscis, ensuring both have a better chance of SURVIVAL!

Flember

PROSPERITY

Do we have the right to control flember, if it is not ours in the first place?

It is a question we MUST answer. Can flember be controlled artificially? If so, should we try?

visible
naturally

DECAY

we
ns
ber,
time
nd
nit
they
mber
rough
fungus
hem.
has
heir
lember
nato
stem.
esses
eping
TREAT
maintain
life

looking at a ghost. Then she stood up straight, walking out from behind the bar and towards the doors. 'All of you, keep eating,' she shouted to the other miners. 'Dev, Boja, you two come with me.'

37
Prosperity

'Boja, if you wouldn't mind?'

Dev stood by the quarry wall, in front of a stacked pile of rusting metal. It was night now, the Garden having taken all day to build, and the food having taken all evening to enjoy.

A chill crept upon the air.

Dev rubbed his arms for warmth.

Boja put down the fourth, fifth and sixth bowls of flonion soup he'd brought with him, then he reached up and started pulling scraps of metal away from the rocky walls.

'This is where we dump things,' Rebecca said.

'Years of broken machines, towers, tools, all left to pile up here. But we chose this spot for a reason.'

She dug the tip of her boot into the crumbly, grey soil. It hit metal.

A length of it, riveted into the ground.

'Tracks!' Dev gasped. He clawed at the mud with his hands, following what looked like railway tracks away from the Garden, through the piles of metal and towards the quarry wall.

crystals used to,' Rebecca said. 'Along these tracks, and then right . . . through . . . *there*.'

As Boja dragged the last few sheets of metal away, they revealed a tunnel carved into the quarry wall.

Dev stepped towards the tunnel and peered into the musty darkness. 'Prosperity? Darkwater dug up all their flemberthysts, and then sent them to *Prosperity*?'

Rebecca nodded. 'For every cart of crystals we sent, we got a cart filled with food in return. Special food, the stuff we couldn't grow here. Breads, meats, jars filled with sweets and pickles. For a while, it was wonderful. Everyone was happy. But when Wilburforce disappeared, the mines stopped working, and we had no more crystals to send.'

She folded her arms defiantly. 'Priest, rest his soul, said Wilburforce had gone back to Prosperity and abandoned us all. So he said we should make Darkwater our own. Persuaded the miners to block this tunnel off. Course, by then the land was dying – nothing was stubborn enough to grow here except for hibbicus – but Priest insisted we make a go of it. Said it was important we stay by the sea.' She sighed a long, pained sigh. 'I didn't believe Wilburforce would just leave us, but what else could I do? If we were going to live here, well then, I'd try to make the Village to feel like a *home*.'

'You did a great job,' Dev said. 'Thank you for looking after us.'

Rebecca smiled. 'Well, thank *you* for bringing us back our flember. I don't think anyone particularly enjoyed my hibbicus stew.'

Dev laughed. 'So we can use this tunnel? Will it take us to Prosperity without having to go through the Wildening again?'

Rebecca nodded.

'Did you hear that, Boja?'

Boja sat, busily slurping through his bowls. 'MMF!' he agreed through a mouthful of flonion soup.

'If you have to go.' Rebecca sighed. 'If you really, really have to go, then this is the safest way.'

'I almost forgot that tunnel was there!' Keeper called out, as she CLANK-CLANK-CLANK-ed towards them on a new set of robot legs.

She came to a stop beside Dev, savouring his stunned expression for a moment. 'Well, you seemed to have the Garden all in hand. So I thought I'd have a rummage through whatever's lying around and . . . y'know . . . fix myself up.'

'We work with what we've got,' Dev cheered.

'Exactly.' Keeper beamed. 'So, you're still looking for

the Flember Stream, then?'

'We are. We *have* to find it.'

'Shame.' Keeper tightened Dev's scarf a little tighter around his neck. 'I was just getting used to you two being around.'

Suddenly there came a clatter of empty bowls from behind them. Dev turned to see Boja, tears welling in his eyes, his arms out wide, as he scooped them all up into a hug so big, so tight, everyone involved had to gasp for air.

'Boja!' Dev croaked.

'FAMILYYYYYY!' Boja sobbed.

It took a fair bit of persuasion, and a few of Keeper's gaskets blowing up Boja's nose, for the huge bear to finally loosen his grip. Everyone took a moment to catch their breath.

'Look after yourselves,' Rebecca finally wheezed. 'I'm sure wherever you go, whatever you do, everyone back in your village will be very proud of you.'

Dev smiled at the thought of it. 'I hope so,' he replied.

'I'm *sure* they will be.' Keeper affectionately patted his arm. 'They're lucky to have you, Dev. Don't stay away from them for too long. Maybe bring them with you next time you visit.'

'We will,' Dev said. He could feel a lump rising in his throat, as he coughed to stifle it. 'Thank you, both, for everything.'

Boja, who had gone back to licking his soup bowls clean as a way to distract himself, dropped them to the ground and shuffled towards the tunnel entrance.

'Ready,' he sniffled.

'Are you sure?' Dev asked, gripping onto his finger.

'Hungry,' Boja replied.

Dev laughed. 'Of course you are. Well then, let's go and see what there is to eat in Prosperity.'

What Happened Next

Once Rebecca had made her way back inside the Garden, Keeper climbed on top of its roof. Her night was not to be spent in the warm. As well as rebuilding her legs, she'd also taken time to boost up her headlamps, rejangling the trobbletrons just like Dev had suggested. Now they beamed brighter than ever, bright enough that they might be seen for miles.

Bright enough to warn the ships away.

She paraded back and forth, Darkwater's very own human/robot beacon, keenly watching for any lights sailing between the reef. It didn't take long, however, for her to notice something else entirely. A noise, not from the sea, but from the quarry wall behind her.

She swung her lights around, shining them up towards the Wildening. They blinded whoever was up there, causing them to slip out and skid down the near vertical drop where they crashed into the piles of rusted metal.

'Sorry!' Keeper shouted, as she slid down from the Garden roof. 'Sorry! Sorry! Oh, FUDDLESTICKS, are you *hurt?*'

She clambered over the old mining vehicles, heaving bits of rusted metal out of the way.

And there she found a *boy*.

His clothes were torn, his body bruised, his hands still gripped tightly around the handle of a wide, heavy sword. He slowly lifted his head, and stared at Keeper through a tangle of floppy, purple hair.

'My name is Santoro Everdew.' He coughed. 'I'm looking for my brother.'

Dev and Boja's adventures continue in

coming soon...

Acknowledgements

A ridiculously huge thank you to everyone who has helped me turn Flember book two into what it needed to be. To Team DFB for all your support, to Sarah for your patience, to Jodie for your advice, to Emily for your incredible work colouring the illustrations and of course to Alison for all your hard work bringing it all to life. And a special thanks to Rosie, for seeing what lay beyond the first draft.